and Hyacinths

An Attic Press Book of Fiction

Edited by

Caroline Walsh

Attic Press
Dublin

First Published in Ireland in 1993 by
Attic Press
4 Upper Mount Street
Dublin 2

British Library Cataloguing in Publication Data is available from the British Library.

ISBN 1-855940-68X

This book is published with the assistance of The Arts Council/An Chomhairle Ealaíon.

Cover Design: Katharine White
Origination: Attic Press
Printing: Leinster Leader Print, Kildare

About the Editor

Caroline Walsh was born in Dublin and reared there and in Co. Meath. She has been a journalist with *The Irish Times* since 1975 and is currently Features Editor there. Caroline edited a collection called *Modern Irish Stories* in 1985 and is the author of *The Homes of Irish Writers* published in 1982. She lives with her husband and children in Dublin.

Contents

Acknowledgements

Many thanks to Conor Brady, Editor of *The Irish Times*, whose idea it was to publish a fiction series in the paper that was to last almost a decade and who, when asked about the notion of devoting one summer entirely to the work of emerging Irish women writers said, 'If you think it's the right thing to do, go ahead.' Thanks also to academic and author Ailbhe Smyth for her invaluable guidance and wonderful enthusiasm for the series.

Finally, thank you to everyone in Attic Press, especially to Gráinne Healy with whom it was both instructive and fun to work on this book.

Introduction

It has been said that 1992 was the year that Ireland came face to face with its own psyche and was forced to start growing up. Certainly the reality of a fourteen-year-old child doomed by the law of the land, albeit mercifully temporarily, to continue with an unwanted pregnancy that had made her suicidal – coupled with the spectacle of a prominent Catholic bishop, with a high public profile for humanity and integrity, admitting that he had turned his back, not only on his own son, but on the woman with whom the boy was conceived, rocked the State like few things had before.

But, most importantly from a woman's point of view, these events also succeeded in putting flesh and blood, the imprint of fact rather than fable, on experiences and emotions that had long been the legacy of Irish women; experiences of sexual abuse, of life-threatening pregnancies, denial, hypocrisy and abandonment. These things were happening – and they weren't just happening in women's minds or in the isolated backwoods of Ireland. They were happening on suburban housing estates and in the inner sanctums of the powerful.

The year before all this (1991) *The Irish Times* had decided to devote its annual fiction series to the work of women writers only. Predictably, some objections were raised. Why didn't the newspaper give over a series exclusively to men's work was one point. Another objection was that a women's series was sexist; that women weren't well served by having their artistic work considered in isolation. Would Molly Bloom's soliloquy benefit from being written by a woman instead of a man, one antagonist to the whole idea wrote, arguing that quality should always be the criterion, not gender. To which the answer could only be that no, the climax to Joyce's masterpiece would not necessarily have been better if written by a woman. But it would have been different.

Women feel and see things in a way that is distinct from men and who would have it any other way?

On a more practical level the quality argument might have some merit if women's work had, over the decades, made it into anthologies and onto the bookshop shelves in the same bulk as that of their male counterparts. But one has only to remember the paucity of female contributions in *The Field Day Anthology of Irish Writing*, now being compensated for through a planned extra volume, or examine any of the main literary collections of the past to see that a gender balance simply didn't exist. The compendiums of women's literary work, the dictionaries of literary biography devoted exclusively to women, are very much a new thing; a phenomenon born out of past neglect.

The chief delight of reading manuscripts for a women's fiction series was watching how, gradually, the threads became interwoven as themes echoed one another in story after story, confirming each other, questioning one another; making a dialogue. Like the Aborigines' songlines, a pattern, a patchwork of coherence, was emerging and it had no beginning and no end. It was a part, albeit a tiny part, of what American academic Ann Owens Weekes[1] called 'an uncharted tradition'; the world of Irish women's writing.

The muted voice of women in the Field Day Anthology perpetuated, feminist and scholar, Ailbhe

Smyth[2] said, the myth that Irish women were incapable of writing anything of significance. In fact, leaving aside the major Irish women writers of the past, and moving to much more modern times, a great deal had been going on in the undertow. In what Smyth has called the 'forbidden well',[3] women were confronting and trying to make sense of the myriad of contradictions, the mass of old oppressions, mixed with revolutionary change, that were their lot.

Reading dozens of new short stories for this collection it was at times quite startling how the same common experience was thrown up again and again. Themes like that of the unwanted baby, be it Katy's unborn baby in Maeve Binchy's 'The Custardy Case' because of whom Father is leaving Mother, or the newborn baby in Liz McManus's 'Midland Jihad' left on the steps outside the locked doors of the church, an 'anorak tucked around him'.

> When I was about fifteen someone buried a dead baby in the corner of a field near us. Nobody let on they knew anything about it. The guards came around all the houses, but the girl had already gone to England,

writes Angela Bourke in 'Deep Down', pulling together a lot of familiar images in a few succinct lines. Children wanted, children not wanted, and the child wanted, had – and then lost like Carmelita's Raymond in 'The Garden of Eden' by Éilís Ní Dhuibhne:

> There were the photographs of course, but only in albums. None out on the sideboard, none displayed with the other photographs on the mantelpiece. They had to get over it. They had to forget.

Another recurrent theme is that of woman as carer; woman as she whose needs come, automatically, second to another's. In this group are Kate in Clairr O' Connor's story 'Hyacinths', giving up her dwindling fertile years to nurse an ageing, alcoholic parent, painfully aware that, driven from the house by her cantankerous father, her gardener lover may have taken with him her last chance of pregnancy, and Catherine in Máiríde Woods's 'Baby, Please Stop Crying'. Wandering the corridor outside her small, sick son's ward, she knows that, like her broken bicycle, she is immobilised,

> tied to years of hospitals and waiting rooms, consultants' appointments and bad news.'

Something besides her banjaxed bicycle was splayed against the buildings's railings, 'its lock broken'.

In these stories there runs the thread of women sexually used and abused by men and the desperation it breeds, desperation like that of Mary Morrissy's narrator in 'Divided Attention', cowering in the undergrowth outside the 'pleasing, symmetrical five windows around an arched doorway' suburban home of the married man in whose life for too long she's been the other woman. But, sometimes even in the same story, as here, there is also the notion of women fighting back, taking control; of women refusing the victim label, working their own way towards empowerment. Emotions often labelled as 'mad' or 'hysterical' are suddenly seen in a new light for the sure, strong emotions that they are.

If self sacrifice – real or imagined – has been one of the main hallmarks of the Irish experience, and a continuous literary theme, the question springs to mind, have women, unconsciously, contributed to this tradition, albeit often from a vantage point of powerlessness; a background of the oppressive triptych of patriarchialism, nationalism and catholicism? Has a legacy been inadvertently handed on of helplessness from which generations of Irish mothers and daughters failed to escape except through occasional wild outbursts of bitterness and rage, all grist to the mill in Ireland, a country where hate has been so much part of the culture?

But just as the past can be reassessed, so the future is there to be written. Nothing is inevitable and the emergence of the non-passive, non guilt-ridden, confident Irish woman in the growing body of Irish women's writing is one of its most exciting characteristics. It brings to mind author Erica Jong's powerful urgings to women writers to be able to move on, not to remain trapped forever in the phase of discovering buried anger.

> The anger has been discovered, unearthed, anatomised and catalogued. It may be a strong propellant to the creation of literature, but it is hardly the only propellant.[4]

The themes of these stories by no means spin on the male/female axis. Just as there are strong relationships between women there is also an exploration of something which Irish psychologist Maureen Gaffney recently suggested the feminist tradition hadn't yet acknowledged: envy between women. It's there in the rivalry and bitterness between Brid and Mary in Moy McCrory's story 'The O'Touney Sisters and the Day of Reckoning'. It's there in Clairr O' Connor's story in the menacing presence of the housekeeper, 'her voice maliciously bright' and in Kate's chance meeting with an old friend, Sylvia, surrounded by the batch of children Kate is beginning to feel the lack of in her own life; a meeting that 'diminished her in some way she couldn't fathom'.

Even in this slim collection much can be gleaned too from the recurrent images that turn up effortlessly on page after page. No shortage here of Our Lady's shrines, of paintings and statues of the Virgin Mary, of Saint Anthony, not to mention miracles and rosary beads; the Vatican, the Pope and Lourdes – and a legacy of shame, guilt and embarrassment as evidenced in, say, Mary Dorcey's 'The Lift Home'. But jumbled up with the old icons and emotions are new images – from obscene phone calls to the fear of AIDS. All human life is here, sometimes, indeed often, presented in the most comic of ways. Those who would suggest that modern women's writing is one long moan in the social realism genre would only have to be pointed towards Ivy Bannister's 'Seduced', Anne Enright's 'Luck be a Lady', Moya Roddy's 'Biddy's Research', and 'The Virgin' by Trudy Hayes for evidence of humour and sheer fun, as a means of exploring the most serious of scenarios.

To say too much more about the stories, which were all part of *The Irish Times* women's fiction series, with a few stories added that had appeared in the paper the previous year, might be to diminish them. They speak for themselves. Hopefully reading them is as enjoyable as was collecting them.

Caroline Walsh
March 1993

Notes:

1. Introduction to *Irish Women Writers: An Uncharted Tradition* by Ann Owens Weekes, University Press, Kentucky, 1990. 2. From report by Katie Donovan of debate on Field Day Anthology at the Irish Writers' Centre Dublin in *The Irish Times*, 27 February 1992. 3. Introduction to Wildish Things: An Anthology of New Irish Women's Writing edited by Ailbhe Smyth. Attic Press 1989. 4. 'Blood and Guts: The Tricky Problem of Being a Woman Writer in the Late Twentieth Century' by Erica Jong in *The Writer on Her Work* edited by Janet Sternburg. Virago Press, 1992.

The Custardy Case

by Maeve Binchy

Bernard knew there was something special about his seventh birthday, because they seemed to be talking about it all the time at home. Mother and Father were very busy always rushing in and out shouting to each other about it. There hadn't been as much fuss since last Christmas with all the comings and goings and doors banging and not knowing where anyone was going to be.

His birthday appeared to be causing even more drama. Every time he came into a room people stopped talking. His Grannie, or his Auntie Helen or Daddy's friend from the office, the very fat lady Katy, also came to see them sometimes. And Mother must be working very hard because Grannie and Auntie Helen kept telling her she was wonderful to be able to give a children's party in the middle of everything, and then at different times Katy would put her arm around him and say that he was a lucky boy so many people loved him. Father didn't say much because he was very busy and not home a lot. Sometimes he had to sleep at the office, he worked so hard.

Bernard had asked Katy did she have to sleep at the office too. For some reason everyone went very silent when he said this. They had looked at each other as if trying to guess the answer. Mother had come to the rescue.

'Not any more, no need for that any more,' Mother had said.

Father had got into a mood then, and had said that

this was about as low as they had got, and that for everyone's sake he had to hope that there was no lower to go.

The birthday party tea was going to be at McDonald's, like everyone else at school did for their birthdays, so he didn't know why they kept talking about the menu. At Gerald's party his mother had taken down a list of what everyone wanted in advance and someone had driven ahead to order it. But that was all. In Bernard's home they kept talking about the food. He couldn't count the number of times he had heard them talking about the custardy case. It must be a new kind of pudding, and a huge secret. Because nobody mentioned the custardy case when he was there, it was only on the phone or when they didn't realise he was in earshot. It must be a difficult pudding because Auntie Helen was saying that there was no knowing which way it would go, and Grannie was saying that these things were usually cut and dried which sounded awful but Mother was saying that there was nothing cut and dried about it at all.

Nobody spoke about the custardy case in front of Father or Katy. Maybe it was a surprise for them too.

Bernard liked Katy even if she waddled a lot. She had a lovely smile and she was interested in his school report and the sports at school. She said she loved the high jump herself. Bernard thought that she was probably far too fat to jump three inches above the ground but didn't say anything of the sort. He nodded sagely as she told him about her school and how they had once put on a gymnastic display.

'Katy's good at the high jump,' he told Mother and Auntie Helen.

'You can say that again,' Auntie Helen said grimly.

'Shush,' Mother had said warningly.

He went out for walks with Father and Katy on Sundays, Mother never wanted to come, but Katy wasn't a bit insulted.

'Your mother has to work very hard, even on Sundays,' she explained. Mother showed people houses for an estate agency. Sometimes couples wanted to see a place at weekends. It was the only time they had free. For as long as he could remember, Mother had to jump up suddenly when the phone rang.

'And don't you have to work any more?' Bernard couldn't quite understand, if Katy had been a friend of Father's in the office, why did she not go there any more? It was no use asking Mother about it after all that strange fuss when he had wondered about Katy sleeping in the office. He thought it better to ask her directly.

Katy didn't seem a bit upset. They were walking together. Father had gone off to get ice cream.

'No, I'm having a baby you see; it's in here.' She held Bernard's hand to her stomach. 'So I can't really go to work any more. It wouldn't be fair.'

'Why wouldn't it be fair?'

'On the baby, and on everyone else.'

'When will it come out?' he looked at Katy fearfully.

'In about two weeks' time.'

'After my birthday!' Bernard was pleased that none of this would interfere with the celebrations. He was going to ask Katy about this case of custard pudding that Mother, Grannie and Auntie Helen were all so het up about. But he didn't. If it was meant to be a surprise then he had better let it be a surprise for him.

Father came back with the three cones.

'Katy's having a baby,' Bernard told him, thinking father would be pleased and interested at this news.

'I know,' Father said in a strange voice. It sounded like as if it was the most extraordinary thing in the world instead of something anyone could do. Harriet, the cat, had four babies last month and the hamsters at school were always having them.

'Could we have a baby at home do you think?' he asked Father. There was another of those silences. Bernard was beginning to find them very irritating. What could be wrong with people when you asked perfectly ordinary questions? Why did they suddenly get struck dumb?

At school next day Bernard told Gerald that Katy was going to have a baby in two weeks. It was nearly ready but not quite. 'Will it be like a brother for you?' Gerald asked. Bernard was puzzled. How could it be like a brother, it was belonging to Katy from the office. He did what he did when he didn't understand things. He gave Gerald a punch in the arm and Gerald gave him a wallop back and soon they were rolling about on the playground.

Miss Hayes separated them. 'What was that about?' she asked. Bernard and Gerald looked at her blankly. They couldn't remember. Miss Hayes believed them. Children often belt each other for no reason. She would have forgotten it if Bernard's mother hadn't called at lunchtime and asked was everything all right with her son. Miss Hayes mentioned the unexpected fight and almost immediately regretted it when she saw the woman's face.

Bernard was pleased to see his mother coming to collect him.

'Can we bring Gerald for an ice cream?' he asked.

'I thought you and Gerald were fighting, like tinkers,' Mother said. Bernard sighed, you couldn't do much without it getting home.

'That was nothing,' he muttered.

'Why did he hit you?' Mother wouldn't have dreamed that Bernard was the aggressor. But Bernard had a very strong sense of justice.

'I sort of hit him first. He said I was having a brother.'

Mother looked very upset. She was biting her lip. Bernard wanted to reassure her, let her know he had sorted it out.

'It's all right. I told him it was Katy that was having the baby not you.' He expected her to be pleased at his grasp of events and his swift action in thumping anyone who got them wrong. To his horror right there in full view of the school, Mother went down on her hunkers and pulled him to her in a terrible bear-like hug.

'I love you so much Bernard, don't ever forget that. You're the dearest, best boy in the whole world.' He knew she was crying.

Bernard wriggled trying to escape, all kinds of people were looking at them. He beat on Mother's shoulders with his free fists begging her to let him go.

When she loosened her arms from around him, he ran off as fast as he could.

He saw Mother standing looking after him but he didn't care. He had to be away from all the people who would laugh at a boy of nearly seven being hugged by a mother kneeling on the road. It was the worst thing that had ever happened to him in his whole life.

When he got home Father was there, which was nice. Father was hardly ever home at this time of the day.

Bernard was pleased when he saw the car outside the door and ran in shouting for him.

Grannie and Auntie Helen were sitting in the kitchen, but Father was upstairs.

There were three suitcases open on the bed. Father was packing, suits and clothes. Bernard's face lit up.

'Are we going on our holidays?' he cried out excitedly.

Father looked very annoyed to see him.

'Your mother said she was picking you up from school. She couldn't even bloody do that. She couldn't keep her word.'

Bernard hated when Father and Mother said bad things about each other. He was going to explain that Mother had been there but he was too interested in the suit cases.

'Where are we going, where Father, please tell me?'

Father sat down on the bed. He looked old and sad suddenly. 'Bernard you weren't meant to be here, you were meant to be out for all this.'

This whole business about surprises was getting very hard to handle. There was the cake at McDonald's, there was this holiday, Bernard wished that people would let him in on things, let him look forward to it, tell people at school about what was happening.

He looked at the cases on the bed. These were the big ones, the ones they had taken to Spain and down to Kerry and they only came down from the attic when it was time to go on a holiday.

'Will I go and pack too, Father?' he asked, hoping that this was the right thing to suggest. Father's face looked a bit grey. Maybe he just needed to be left on his own for a bit. To Bernard's utter horror, Father suddenly grabbed him in exactly the same awful hug that Mother had.

'Oh Bernard, I wouldn't have had this happen for the world,' he said into Bernard's hair. And Bernard tried to fight the thought but he really believed that Father was crying too. He escaped just as he had done from Mother and got to his own room.

Bernard had got an early birthday present from Katy. It was a super Walkman, and a little plastic rack for holding tapes. Katy had said that it could be nailed up on a wall wherever he was and that he would always have his tapes near him and he could listen to them whenever he wanted to. Bernard had explained that Mother had said things shouldn't be nailed on the wall but he'd put it beside the bed. It kept falling over. He wished Mother hadn't said that about not nailing it to the wall, as Katy had said what were old walls for anyway except to put things on.

He listened to his tapes, and wondered about the holiday and where it would be, and whether Katy would come too, and would the baby be ready while they were on holidays, and would Miss Hayes mind, and what day they'd come back to be in time for the birthday.

He lay on his bed with his eyes closed and he thought he saw Grannie and Auntie Helen come in and go out, and he heard Mother's voice, but it was arguing with Father's, so he turned up the volume, and since it was only his own ears, nobody else could get annoyed by it and come and tell him to turn it down. Sometimes when he was changing the tapes he heard Mother crying and Father shouting, and though he could hardly believe it, they were still talking about the party and the pudding and who was going to order it or collect it or get it.

Mother was saying that a man never got custardy, never in the history of the whole thing. Father was saying it wasn't a man; it was ready-made family; it was people who would stay at home all day and mind children, not gallivanting off with every Tom, Dick and Harry who waltzed into an estate agency looking for an outing.

Mother was saying that some of the judges were women nowadays; they weren't medieval any more, they knew a woman could work and mind a child.

Father said judges were judges whatever sex they were. They could see where the advantage lay. They weren't fools. Bernard now saw that there was going to be some kind of competition, a cookery competition involved about the custard puddings. Everything pointed to it, there could be no other explanation.

He went into the room, where the suitcases were now on the floor and where Mother and Father were both crosser than he had ever seen them in their lives.

'I don't mind about the pudding,' Bernard said with the air of a man who had solved it all.

'Let's have no pudding, no custardy case at all.'

They stood looking at him, it was like a freeze-frame on the television, or when you press the pause button.

He knew that none of them would ever forget this minute but he had no idea why.

It kept coming back to him in the days that followed, the days when everyone seemed to have stopped talking like they used to talk. There had been no holiday; of course that was a false alarm. And there had been no pudding on his birthday at McDonald's, but nobody thanked him for his solution to that one. And Katy's baby got ready and came out and was a girl, and Father was very pleased, and said he'd better stay with Katy a lot more to look after things because he wasn't able to stay in the old place anymore. He never called it home; he always called it the old place.

And there were all the conversations with other people, lawyers, and Mother got more and more tired because she had to work so hard and Auntie Helen and Grannie got very cross and snapped the nose off everyone.

And Bernard still remembered the freeze-frame feeling on the day that he went to court and the judge said he wanted to see him in his chambers. Bernard knew that chambers didn't mean what you thought it would mean, but he didn't know it was going to be an ordinary room.

And the judge was nice. Bernard told him all about Mother having to work so hard and never being at home, and how hard it was to talk to Mother because of Grannie and Auntie Helen being there and being so cross. The judge seemed to know that kind of thing, and he was very interested when Bernard explained about not being able to nail things on the wall, and Mother kneeling down and crying outside the school. The judge asked about Katy and Bernard said that it was amazing how thin she had got when the baby was ready and came out, and Katy often had said that he, Bernard, was a lucky boy because so many people in the world loved him.

And no, Katy had never said a word against Mother. She had said that Mother was terrific but worked too hard, and was never there when you were looking for her which Bernard, struggling to be fair, said was true.

And afterwards there was a lot of noise outside, and Grannie and Auntie Helen were saying terrible things to Katy and Father. Mother was very quiet and said nothing. Katy said that she had invited Bernard's friend, Gerald, to come and stay for a few days, and she had put up lots of shelves and racks for them on the wall.

Bernard couldn't understand why they seemed to think he wasn't going home. He must be going to stay with Katie and Father and the new baby girl. He didn't know how long the visit would be for, but he thought it better not to ask.

Then Mother said she'd come to see Bernard on Saturday. About eleven o'clock, and they'd go somewhere nice. Mother's eyes looked very strange, as if there was no light in them any more.

She hardly waved when he got into the car with Father and Katy. She just kept looking in front of her as if she didn't see anything at all.

Baby, Please Stop Crying

by Máiríde Woods

The lock is jammed. Catherine twists it, jiggles it, reforms the numbers, but it remains obstinately shut, clamping her borrowed bicycle to the railings. Tears slide down cheeks. Since Kit has been in hospital, she is an absolute fountain, every silly predicament making her cry. How will she explain about the bicycle when she gets back to her aunt's house? Her aunt is fussy about possessions. And she will have to ring Phil tonight and tell him what the consultant said. Her aunt is fussy about her phone bill too ...

Perhaps the hall-porter would help. Catherine peered into the hospital lobby with its diamond patterned tiles but the friendly one hadn't come on duty. The red-faced man presently doing time in the cubby-hole, didn't like bicycles. He'd already told her to move hers twice, said it lowered the tone of the hospital to have bikes chained to the front railings, felt that real parents arrived in cars or taxis ... Catherine tried the combination again, this time as gently as possible. God, if you make this work, she began, then stopped. If God hadn't listened to her prayers about Kit, it wasn't likely he'd bestir himself over an old lock.

'Something wrong?' the man asked.

'My lock has jammed,' Catherine said, averting her face to hide the tears.

The man knelt down on the mossy tarmacadam.

'Tell me the number,' he said.

'7324,' she told him. He formed the numbers in a masterful way, but nothing happened.

'Are you sure you have the number right?' he asked. Catherine nodded despite a moment of doubt. But 73 was the number of her aunt's house, and 24 her age.

The man shook the lock. Catherine saw that he wanted to escape but was reluctant to be bested by an inanimate object. Phil would be like that too, she thought.

'Are you a visitor?' he asked.

'Yes,' she said. 'And yourself?'

She recognised his smile of fellow feeling.

'I'll wait for the nice porter,' she told him. 'The one in there now is an ogre.'

'Most of them are ogres here,' the man said.

And it was true. St Killian's was an annexe to the Children's Hospital, and served as a dumping ground for difficult staff.

He stood there undecided. Catherine noticed that he was a nice-looking man with brown eyes and ruffled sort of hair. In another life she might have tried to flirt with him, get off with him even ...

'Would you like a drink?' he asked suddenly. 'There's a pub just around the corner.'

Catherine jumped. She was about to say, no, I'm married, my child is in hospital but the words were too ridiculous ...

'Come on,' he said. 'It'll be another hour before the shift changes. You might as well.'

She found herself walking down the dark avenue and turning into a cosseted suburb full of ornamental trees. But the curtains were drawn and the bare twigs dripped February rain. She was conscious of the man's green anorak brushing against her red one. Swish, swish. If it had been Phil, she would have been hoping he'd take her hand, judging his mood, trying to please

... It was a long time since she had been walking with a man other than Phil. Funnily, with a stranger she felt freer.

He held the door of the pub open and as the noise and the lights hit Catherine, she felt unreal. Yet she had been in a pub only two nights ago. She had put on her make-up and high heels and gone out with some of the girls from her old office. Surrounded by gins and vodkas she had drunk a little too much, giggled and chattered, pretended to look at fellows ... But most of the girls had steady relationships now; some were married, some had babies ... It was when they got to the babies that she had to totter out to the loo. All their babies had accomplishments. Not like Kit. In the end she had left early, having spent most of her week's allowance. She had forgotten how expensive Dublin was.

'If you think Kit needs you, stay,' Phil had said, when they brought him to St Killian's first. They hadn't realised that the tests would take three weeks. She checked her money. Would it be safer to pay for her drink or would the man be offended? He put a hot whiskey in front of her before she had made up her mind.

'The name's Alan Conroy,' he said, beaming. She smiled remembering how she used to be with men; like a blackbird, trying out her finest notes, wheedling little bits of information from them, teasing them ... Four years ago when she had never been inside a hospital. Four years ago when she could have told any hospital porter to fuck off ...

'I think I saw you up in Blessed Imelda's,' Alan said.

'My son is there,' Catherine said.

'My daughter was in that ward, two years ago,' the

man told her. 'They always have the toddlers there. How do you find the sister?'

'She's a head-case,' Catherine said. 'The nurses are all scared of her – and so am I. So far she has been nice to me – but it's like being embraced by a lobster.'

He laughed and Catherine felt uneasy. She hadn't quite figured out why the sister was considerate, and she felt uncertain about the word 'embrace.' Was it provocative, a come-on? Oh, come on, she told herself, four years married and you've dwindled into a mouse. And she thought again of Kit.

Alan didn't ask her what was wrong with Kit and she was grateful. Mostly St Killian's got tests or convalescent cases. In Blessed Imelda's there were six toddlers – and Mary Crinion. Most of the two year-olds were recovering from chest infections and Catherine found it difficult to understand their parents' anxieties, for in spite of being tied into their cots for most of the day, they were getting better. The other mothers didn't understand about Kit either. With his rosy cheeks and his smile, he seemed perfectly healthy. But there was the spectre of Mary Crinion at the end of the ward – Mary who was eight, but couldn't walk or talk very well, Mary whom nobody visited.

Until today there had been no definite news about Kit. For ten days Catherine had lain in wait for the consultant and today she had almost collided with him. While the hands of the clock moved between 9.52 and 9.55 he had told her in the irritated, abstracted way he had with parents. She had kept her eyes on the fresh stain which ran from his paisley tie to the lapel of his suit. Some child must have thrown up over him, she thought, when he let himself get too close.

'I'll send the final report to your own doctor,' he

finished, hurrying away.

I should ring Phil, she thought, fingering the change in her pocket. Alan was talking about last Saturday's rugby match. Phil knows, she told herself, Doctor O'Driscoll warned us what to expect. What is the point of all these blood samples and EEGs then? Better to have a name put on it, Phil had said. You must trust the doctors, Aunt Anne kept repeating.

Now Alan was talking of the Dublin bombing of last year. We were happy then, Catherine thought guiltily, unreasonably, we didn't know ... And once again she found tears sneaking down her cheeks. She shook her long dark hair forward to hide them. She used to be so proud of her hair; she would iron it going to the hops; and Phil used to finger it admiringly. Nowadays she barely remembered to wash it. Other images haunted her, broken bodies, children like Mary Crinion.

'It's terrible seeing the kiddies just lying in their cots,' Alan was saying. 'I don't know why they can't let them out a bit more. My little one has got very withdrawn, even though we've been in to see her every day. What must it be like for children from the country?'

'Unimaginable,' Catherine said, thinking of three-year-old Michael.

And at the same time it was so ordinary that nobody minded. Michael was from Offaly and had been admitted ten days ago. He had been crying ever since. In the morning his pillow was wet, at breakfast the tears ran into his cornflakes. All his Ladybird books had become mushy, and his teddy looked as if it had been through the washing machine. The sister had spoken sharply to him, the doctor had jollied him, Catherine and the student nurses had tried to play games with him, the cleaning lady had carried him all the way down the corridor to see if his mammy was coming. None of it made any difference. Michael went on crying. And the awful thing was, thought Catherine, that you accommodated to it. It became ludicrous, out of proportion, irritating even.

'What's he got to cry about?' grumbled a surgeon who was famous for his work on bomb victims.

'Still crying, Mikey,' the nurses would ask every time they passed.

Kit didn't cry. He seemed quite happy to sit in his cot. He didn't even mind the tests very much. It was hard to know if he missed Catherine at night. It was hard to know anything about Kit.

'There's a kid in Blessed Imelda's who cries all the time,' Catherine told Alan.

'Where are his parents?' he asked.

'He's from Birr, like me,' she said. They have a pub and other children. They can't stay.'

'You're from the country, then,' he said.

'Yes,' Catherine said. 'I'm staying with relatives. I'm lucky to be able to do that.'

It was lucky that she had Aunt Anne to put her up in the neat red-brick house in Rathgar. Aunt Anne couldn't deal with the tidings Catherine brought home from the hospital though. She retreated into fussing over meals and her son's bicycle and young people not going to Mass.

'Have you other children?' the man asked.

'No,' she replied, 'I'm lucky that way too.'

It was lucky since it meant she could stay with Kit; yet in Birr most girls had their first couple of babies close together. Kit will be spoiled, Phil's parents told her and she felt her power to choose diminishing, the mesh of motherhood closing over her head.

'Ah well, you're young,' Alan was saying, 'you've plenty of time yet.' He smiled at Catherine, and she realised how old he was. He probably only asked me to have a drink because he felt sorry for me, she thought, as another tear slid treacherously down her cheek.

'I'd just hate to have a whole lot of kids one after another,' she said, tossing her head. 'Phil and I always said we'd have our family well spaced out.'

They hadn't, of course; they hadn't discussed it at all. She had gone on the pill, and Phil had said, fine, darling ... Perhaps he would have liked another ... Perhaps it would have helped now ...

'Ours are spread out,' the man was saying. 'There's the little one inside who's five, then a lad of ten, then the big fellow of fifteen. We got a great kick out of the little one,' he went on quietly and Catherine knew that whatever was wrong wasn't trivial. But she couldn't bring herself to ask. Another sad story, and she'd be howling openly in this bright night-time pub. Baby, please stop crying, Phil used to say to her in his mock-Bob Dylan voice. It had been a joke for in those days she never cried. But Phil wasn't here, he was back in Birr, studying for his accountancy exam in his old bedroom in his parents' house. She hated to think of their own little house being empty, but Phil could see no point in staying there on his own.

'You shouldn't have been in such a hurry to get married,' Aunt Anne had said more than once – Aunt Anne whose own daughters had planned their weddings years in advance. Catherine had to bite her tongue, be circumspect, for Kit's sake, for the sake of their finances. It wasn't that Aunt Anne was unkind but her way of making clucking noises over other people's lives was hard to bear.

They sipped the last of the hot whiskey. A wild idea came to Catherine. There was still time to catch the last bus to Birr, take Michael home to his mother and stop his agonised crying; go home to Phil herself. She looked at Alan. Could she tell him? No, he would think she was one of those mad women who steal babies from prams; he would inform the hospital, and she and all her seed and breed would be disgraced forever and ever ... Yet how could it be right to leave Michael crying?

'I'll have to go,' Alan was saying. 'Will you be all right?'

She nodded.

'What about your husband?' he asked tentatively. 'Maybe he should be here with you ...'

'He can't get away from work,' Catherine said. 'He has exams coming up. And nobody can ever tell how long tests will take, or when the consultant will come – or anything.'

The man looked at the rain-marks on his shoes.

'I know,' he said, ' I've had years of it.'

And Catherine thought again, I must ring Phil. I should be sharing this with Phil, not with a stranger. Yet on Sunday nights when Phil set off back to Birr in the old Triumph, she could sense the relief in him ... He was lucky to have his work; he could immerse himself in figures. He was doing liquidations at the moment ... other people's tragedies, Catherine thought, always easier to bear than one's own. She wished she had work. There was so little she could do with Kit in the hospital. And she didn't even trust his lovely smile any more. Maybe it was only a reflex.

'I'm sorry about your daughter,' she said to Alan as they left the pub.

He turned up the collar of his anorak.

'Just one of those things,' he said. 'I'll bring a pair of wire cutters tomorrow evening. If all else fails, we can use them.'

'You're very kind,' Catherine faltered. She felt guilty, knowing she wouldn't be there, that she would have to run away with Mikey, and to hell with the silly lock.

• • •

Catherine is walking up the dark avenue past the ornamental shrubs, the weeping willows and the Keep-off-the-grass signs. It's past visiting hours and there's nobody round. She might almost be back in the country, except for the growl of the traffic. I'm only 24 she thinks, I should be out dancing, not sitting in a ward of crying children. I should be at home in bed with my husband, not worrying about this stupid lock.

As she climbed the stairs to Blessed Imelda's, she got the characteristic smell of the hospital – a mixture of ancient soup, faintly backed by disinfectant and urine. Will Michael come with me, she wondered? He came down the fire escape to see the stray kitten, she told herself. But that had been in the daylight ...

In Blessed Imelda's the strip-lighting was on, – and – Michael was sitting on another woman's knee, his arms wound round her neck, still crying. Sister's high voice was audible even though Catherine could only see her back.

'Sudden visits upset children. If you can't come regularly, you would be better not to come at all.'

Catherine didn't hear the reply.

'Well that's no concern of mine,' Sister was saying. 'This child was perfectly all right until you turned up this evening. It would be very foolish to leave before the tests are complete.'

She stomped down the ward to Mary Crinion who was making snuffling sounds. Catherine slipped in. She tipped Michael's mother on the shoulder.

'I only have an hour,' the woman said apologetically. 'I got a lift up with a neighbour. I don't know what to do with him, he won't leave go of me.' And she tried ineffectually to detach Michael.

'Take him away,' Catherine whispered. 'It's not true what Sister says. He cries all the time. Take him home.'

She heard Sister's angry footsteps and she retreated to Kit's cot. How untroubled he looked. She kissed him regretfully but he didn't stir so she slipped out through the toilets. Her heart was racing and there were the inevitable tears on her cheeks. I'd never have managed to take Michael away, she thought. I wouldn't have had the courage. And she fingered Kit's little coat which she had intended putting on him as she passed the blue lamp of Our Lady's shrine.

Down in the hall the friendly porter was folding his evening paper.

'How are you, child?' he called. 'You're late tonight.'

And Catherine told him about the lock, and he said he would find her a lift and keep an eye on the bike for her.

'Us country ones have to look after each other,' he said winking. Michael's mother came staggering down the stairs carrying the little boy and various bags and teddies. As Catherine went to help she stole a glance at Michael. His cheeks were still damp but he gave a watery smile.

'I hope I'm doing the right thing,' his mother said. 'The doctor'll have a fit next time he has tonsillitis.'

Sister descended holding a plastic bag with the tips

of her fingers. She handed it to the woman without a word, and went back upstairs.

'I thought she'd eat me,' Catherine said to the porter.

'With some mothers she's afraid,' he said.

Catherine heard a sound up above, and, looking up through the mahogany bannisters saw Sister leading Mary Crinion towards the kitchen. Mary was making gurgling noises.

Catherine remembered the silly plan she had had to rescue Michael and felt as if she had been unfaithful to Kit. But he was asleep in the iron cot upstairs unaware of all her agonising, 'I'll never leave you, Kit,' she vowed, wiping her eyes.

'She's not really such a hard woman,' the porter said gesturing upwards. 'Every night she takes that poor girl down to the kitchen for hot chocolate.'

People did their best, Catherine thought. It wasn't their fault if that wasn't enough. She smiled at the porter.

'Did you get to see your doctor?' he asked.

'For about two minutes,' she said. 'The news isn't good.'

He sighed.

'You'll be going home then?' he said.

'We have to wait for one more test,' Catherine told him, and she thought with a rush of longing of her little house on the Nenagh road. She would light the fire, put on the kettle, and scatter Kit's toys around for company.

The porter came out of his cubby-hole and patted her shoulder.

'You'll have other kids,' he said. 'A whole houseful of them before you're finished. It'll be easier then.'

She looked around the tiled hall at the portraits of

ugly benefactors and her eyes fixed on a nineteenth-century nun. In those days there wouldn't have been any tests she thought. She tried to visualise a houseful of children but couldn't see their faces.

I'll just give that bloody lock one more try, she thought and went out and shone the bicycle lamp on the numbers. She could see them winking, taunting her, telling her that like the bicycle she was immobilised, tied to years of hospitals and waiting rooms, consultants' appointments and bad news. I should ring Phil, she thought, but she knew she wouldn't, she'd wait till tomorrow evening when he was clear of his parent's house, when he belonged to her and Kit again.

• • •

Catherine is walking down the drive to where the porter's friend is to pick her up. The branches of the cypresses flail around in the wind, and rain blows into her face. Even when she is home again this avenue will be inextricably bound up with her worst fears; she will see it every time Kit fails to pass what the books call milestones. And she knows that not even Phil and the promised houseful of children can cancel out the tears she is shedding now. Something besides her cousin's bicycle is splayed against the railings, its lock broken.

The O'Touney Sisters and the Day of Reckoning

by Moy McCrory

My mother wouldn't go out of the house without Saint Anthony of Padua. Not since the time he had saved her from drowning in a bog.

'It's not every day a saint reaches out and plucks you from the jaws of hell,' she always said.

She kept him in her handbag. A travelling Saint Anthony, no bigger than a lipstick, he fitted into his own case.

The first time she left Ireland, newly married to my father, he was the saint who accompanied her on the journey to the godless land.

'He didn't stop me being seasick,' she told us. 'He hasn't the cure at all. Still, I wouldn't be without him.' Her arthritic fingers would stroke the slim metal case inside which the quiet silver statue nestled. He was the perfect travelling companion and the two of them went everywhere together.

My mother believed until her death that she owed her life to him. She was a devout Catholic whose faith was never shaken, unlike her sister who was an atheist. That, in any case, is what my mother called my aunt, although it's hard to see how she could be described as such. Brid never stopped believing in God, it was just that she hated him.

Each summer throughout my childhood we returned to Roscommon and my mother would no sooner have set foot in the old kitchen, but the rows between her and Brid would start.

She was always telling my aunt to mend her ways, to save her soul before it was too late. But Brid was adamant.

'You and your Saint Anthony,' she'd say. 'He might have pulled you clear, but he'd only strength enough for one of us,' and she used to gaze out of the back window towards the distant hills, where sky and earth touched briefly.

'Go on, you heathen. You're walking around alive today,' my mother would scold her. But Brid just said it was a funny sort of life at that.

'What have I ever done?' she'd ask. 'I've never been anywhere. I don't get to see foreign places.'

Once the priest was arranging a visit to Fatima, but knowing my aunt's views on religion he did not offer her the chance.

'You can stay with us whenever you like,' my mother always remonstrated. And Brid would ask who was going to keep house for Titus when she was away. 'It's all right for you,' she always said, 'you and your Saint Anthony.'

Brid was my spinster aunt. She kept house for her brother. There had been, before I was born, a time when Uncle Titus was walking out with the tailor's daughter. It came to nothing. My mother said Brid had a hand in the business. She could not have tolerated another woman in the kitchen.

I grew up hearing different stories about the Anthony of Padua rescue. Brid always referred to it as 'The Day Liddy Marnoch Gave Hospitality'. This was my great aunt. An old photograph and a reputation for meanness were all I knew of her.

'God, but she'd not give you a drop of tea if you'd had your throat cut.'

On her stinginess they were all agreed. It was said that she'd serve up plain boiled potatoes and hide the salt so that no one would have the taste for more than a couple.

'It was a penance going to visit her,' Titus used to say.

Their mother, my grandmother, had quarrelled with Liddy and used to yell that she would not have any of them going to see 'that woman'. She would not use her name.

'Why your uncle Jack married her is a mystery,' she would say. 'She's no aunt to any of you, all she ever wants you for is cheap labour.'

Usually they only went to the house if they knew their uncle might be home, otherwise Liddy would have them working around the house for her. But then, she had no one to help around the place. In one yellowed photograph that survives of her she is a thin unsmiling woman, as tight as a bit of flax. Her womb inherited her meanness so that her household would always have to rely on hired labour.

And Liddy was houseproud – always busy with a routine of polishing and dusting, of sweeping and washing. She never stood still for a moment as, with elbow grease, she rubbed out the emptiness of her days. They all agreed that even her kitchen was like a palace and I would imagine it to be like one of the great ruined castles we were brought out to see during the holidays. It must have felt a cold, hard place like the ancient seats of the kings of Ireland that were long empty, their subjects dispossessed, their winding cries left to sound against ruined walls and echo down the hollow years. And freezing. Liddy never lit the hearth until it was time for Jack to come home. She said it was a waste of good turf just for herself, but she'd watch visitors shivering and never light a stick for their comfort. The only time the kettle was put on was at the sound of his boots.

It wasn't reticence had her this way. My father once told me that her cake, whenever you were lucky enough to get a bit, was the best in the county. And her bread they described in unison as being more like scone, but she kept it under lock and key in the press and would only bring in a few slices at a time. They said it was a marvel to see how she could spread a piece and still keep a knife full of butter. How she managed to cut bread so thin was an art she had developed over the years.

'If you held it up to the window you could see your hand through it,' Titus said.

On the day of the disputed miracle, my mother and aunt, both young girls then, had set out to walk to Liddy's. Knowing they'd get nothing until Jack arrived home they took with them a bottle of cold tea and some soda bread to keep them going. It was Brid's idea. Deep down, my mother said, Brid was good-hearted, thinking to pay her miserly aunt a call. But Titus always muttered about the farmhands. He told me Brid was the better looking then and according to his version it was the want of a husband that prompted the charitable visit.

They all said that the weather had been terrible. They had never seen rain like it before or since. The land was soft and spongy from so much moisture. One of the stories my mother told me was of a terrible wet summer when people thought the sea was swallowing the land. Not a day went past throughout two weeks, and some said two months, that was not saturated.

Old people pummelled rosary beads and worried, but said nothing lest their families called them fools. And when it stopped they were scared to trust the new dryness as reeds and grasses hissed and the earth steamed. They were nervous to jab the fragile blue with sudden movement when the sky was so thin that a flock of birds might tear it. The elderly waited indoors and let the eager and the young test the day.

All her life my mother was solid and sturdy, but Brid was slight. In old photographs she looks wispy. She had dressed with special care that day. Titus always laughed over the attentions she once lavished on herself. The care she took of her appearance was legendary and for that walk she carried a pair of dainty sandals in her pocket and wore plimsolls, while my mother strode out determinedly in stout walking boots.

Brid used to say that she was cut out for better things. She had her eye on the distance, dreaming of America. My mother said she would follow her. They were, until then, inseparable, great friends, always in the thick of things, according to uncle Titus. But to me they were always distant with each other, the remnants of sisterhood only present in their furious arguments.

As they approached the farm they saw their uncle's rick disappear and Liddy at the open door in her apron.

'Jesus! Get down!' Brid yelled to my mother who was standing, innocently, to wave.

'Don't let her see us! We'll be called in to scrub the floor or worse. She'll have us worked to death before Uncle Jack comes back. I've me best clothes on, I'm not getting them ruined.'

The two bent their heads and crept off, continuing down the lane until the house was nothing but a smudge in the distance.

'We'll go up later, when Jack is back. Then she might give us tea.'

It was a fine day despite the previous weeks of rain. It was hot and the ground was drying out. They spread out their cardigans and lay back, watching the sky.

'I don't want to get covered in grass stains. What's my hair like, Mary?' Brid asked.

My mother couldn't understand why her sister was so fussed. But Titus knew. There was a farmhand their uncle Jack said would go a long way. Titus would nod at me, but never say more. Once he told me he was the sort of fellow who saved up his money.

'He was what you might call sensible. A man with plans for himself.'

But my mother was unaware of their lives moving on, of futures that were to be decided. She thought then that her girlhood might last for ever.

That afternoon long ago they played. The ghosts of girls ran across the hills and cast shadows on the land, unaware of the darkest; the big soft bog at the bottom of the hollow.

Nestled between a crescent of slopes lay a treacherous patch of ground that was shifting and liquid. They ran down one of the slopes which turned into this and tumbled wildly, out of control, laughing.

Brid was the first to sink.

As she felt herself drop she yelled to her sister to go back, but Mary could not stop and followed her straight in, up to the ankles.

Brid pulled her feet, but could not move them against the weight of earth, a great oppressive richness which held her fast. The heavy wetness pressed down as all around her the earth opened, to suck like a voracious mouth and close against her skin.

She flailed and thrashed, and sank further with each gesture of despair. Her calves were buried, but she would not stop struggling.

'Do something! Do something!' she shouted to her silent sister. Mary obediently began to scream.

They exhausted themselves with shouting. They yelled and howled, they pleaded, they begged. Their voices rang in that out-of-the-way place where no one ever went. Marsh-hoppers and dragon flies ignored them. A crow turned its head towards them, then looked away, and a solitary hare thrashed against the bracken on the outer ground before diving back into the darkness of leaves. It was hopeless. Brid wept as her legs disappeared. Around them insect life hummed and continued undisturbed. Mary began to pray.

'Is that the best you can do?' Brid screamed as she struggled to push herself forward to the slope in the vain hope of catching at some long stems of grass.

'Prayers are useless. We need action, not words!'

Her voice was high and piercing and she continued to shout hoarsely as she moved with agonised slowness. Each effort caused her to sink further.

Mary was rigid. She turned her face to heaven and the only movement from her was that of her lips mouthing an intercession to Saint Anthony, the patron of lost things.

Brid was desperate; swearing and yelling she continued to writhe and turn from the waist. She beat the surface of the bog with her fists, crying and wailing now that the soft ground had pulled her down as far as her thighs.

She knew she was gong to die. Shouldn't her life flash in front of her? Shouldn't she make peace with God? And the sky was blue, it wasn't a day to die. Then she heard her sister shouting joyously.

'We're saved! We're saved! He'll get us out. Glory be to God, we're saved!'

'Where?' Brid shielded her eyes against the empty sky and saw nothing. Mary was fidgeting in her skirt pocket. Did she have a piece of rope or what?

Brid watched in amazement as her triumphant sister drew out her little capsule of Saint Anthony and held it up to heaven. The silver case flashed in the sunlight while Mary's lips moved in silent supplication.

'You omadhaun! Gombhean!' Brid was hysterical with impotent rage as the vision of her sister rose next to her, erect with her one hand towards the sky and her blue eyes lit by the sun, chanting the joyful mysteries.

'You great fool! This isn't Lourdes!' she screamed.

Brid knew that even if it had been, if they were sinking in some holy place, right in front of the altar and not in this god-forsaken spot away from everything, nothing would save them but their own wits. Even if they were to drown in the middle of the Vatican with the Pope looking on, all that could save them would be mortal intervention.

That was when she realised that the immortals were powerless. The sky was empty and only hands, solid and real hands, could haul them out. Prayers went nowhere, spent on empty air, just as their pleas for help had done.

And she knew the fault was theirs. They ought to have known the lay of the land, they ought to have recognised the signs, but earth disguises itself, even taking in farmers.

Buffer Kierney had lost a heifer in sinking soil, and once a commercial traveller passing though, parked his car in a field after a rainstorm while he warmed up in Dummican's lounge. He never saw it again.

Now Brid's waist was level with the ground. She wiggled like some crawling maggot. Mary felt her calves slip down further.

'Blessed Saint Anthony, help us in our hour of trial,' Mary prayed while Brid spat and cursed, and fought the land.

It was claiming them still living. Without decency the earth was opening into graves. It croaked its desire, without respect or dignity. Indecorously it held on while Brid twisted first one way and then the other in helpless rage.

Each move carried her further into the treacherous sinking soil. Soil that was water-drenched where the sea lapped, where it seeped below the crust of earth they walked on every day without knowing. They were being pulled back to stay preserved with the forests and the tiny impressions of fossils, the print of a creature that had lived before the lands separated, before humankind stood upright. Down into ageless earth which nursed their past, hugged all of life to itself and to which they would surely return. They were being pulled down to lie along the unmarked famine graves, sinking to press upon the layers of battlefields, of warriors, of cattle raids and ritual burials. Sinking to add to the unwritten deeds, down among the carbon that was once part of the great wooden doorway, the massive square lintels, and the place where the storyteller sat.

But it was a bright, clear day; not a good one for taking a place in history. The two sisters held onto life with a desperation new to them and struggled against the promise they would one day keep with the earth. Brid fought a stern, material battle while Mary exhausted her soul with praying.

'Wait there!' a man's voice shouted.

Wasn't it one of the farmhands?

'Praise be to God!' Brid yelled, her heresy forgotten. 'We're saved! We're saved!'

Tears poured down her face. Hysterical laughter bubbled in her chest. Already she had glimpsed the future. It was fate that brought them together in this desolate spot. Of all people to pass, but it should be that one. Him. She'd be making the crossing all right, herself and him together. She sobbed with relief.

Mary seemed unaware of anything, even danger was forgotten as she prayed. She continued her litany calmly while the farmhand backed the cart up and tied a length of rope behind. He threw this first to Brid who had sunk past her waist. She grabbed it and clung on as he slowly guided the horse.

The earth squelched, sucked and tore at her, then heaved its prize up ungracefully. Brid shrieked with fear as she felt herself come free. The rope dragged against her hands and the reeds cut her as she was pulled clear of the bog, up onto the slope.

She lay panting and shaking with fright. She had lost both shoes and her skirt, and was stinking of the brown mud, embarrassed in only her slip and blouse.

She watched her sister who was by now up to her knees in the bog, but still upright and dignified, holding the silver capsule out.

They always said she must have looked like a saint in ecstasy and would laugh. It seemed that Mary had to be called twice before she heard her name. Then she too took the rope and later lay on the bank next to her sister. She had lost a shoe.

The young man was sweating from the exertion and the heat. Mud from the cart-wheels had splattered him. Mary's legs were coated up to her knees with stuff. She looked at them all and began to laugh, holding her skirt away so that it did not become further damaged. The hem was already ringed with brown. The farmhand began to laugh with relief. Brid cried and moaned as she attempted to straighten her slip over her legs, but it clung to them. Only the little silver capsule was untouched by earth, it alone shone clean and pure, while even the slope was cut into groves from the wheels of the trailer, and the horse's flanks heaved and glistened.

Brid was unable to speak, or even look at the farmhand. Where she ought to have been grateful, she was only mortified, now that she was clear of danger. He must have seen her behaving like a madwoman, thrashing about and swearing. And now look at her, sitting in her slip like a great hussy, her face all tear streaked and mud everywhere. She had lost her best skirt. Then she remembered that her good sandals were in the pockets. There was no consoling her. She wailed all the way to the house.

They arrived at Liddy's sitting on the back of the cart. They waited outside while their aunt brought them kettles of hot water and they washed themselves out in the bit of yard at the back of the house. Their clothes were ruined. That was the day when mean Liddy Marnock was forced to give them hospitality.

She brought out the oldest clothes she could find for them to wear. Brid sulked all afternoon in an old mac and a pair of her uncle's wellingtons, while Mary, her legs clean, went barefoot and prattled on about Saint Anthony with a shining face.

After washing, the farmhand cut huge slices of bread and made tea, and Liddy's eager eyes watched and counted each slice as it disappeared down the ravenous young gullets of Mary and their hired help.

Brid sat away from them, and had no appetite. She said very little, just grunted in reply to questions. Her legs were cut and bleeding, great purple bruises were appearing.

All afternoon, they sat in Liddy's kitchen, drinking tea and consuming entire loaves. Mary talked on happily and even Liddy had to laugh at the antics of the farmhand to amuse, as he waited on them, paying particular attention to Mary.

When he returned, the first thing Uncle Jack did was to make the sign of the cross that they were both saved, but even he had to laugh at the way Mary recounted the story. He could tell already that it was destined to become one of the good tales for the dark nights: 'How Mary's faith remained unshaken'. But outside his house others told: 'How Liddy was forced to be generous'.

After that, Brid seemed to age quickly. She outgrew the young figure in the photographs. They must have soon become as dated as they are to me now. She was no longer the same laughing girl. It wasn't even that she changed so much physically, she always remained slim, but after that afternoon there was a tiredness about her. It was as if she had been worn away just as a wooden kneeler in church becomes indented with the shape of people's knees, and so retains the memory of prayers. Brid carried an impression with her from that day.

They said that it was as if some of Liddy's bitterness had rubbed off onto her. There's a saying about eating the bread of sourness. Brid, for all her lack of appetite, must have swallowed it that afternoon.

Everyone had a slightly different version of the story. They gave less importance to Saint Anthony of Padua, or more, according to their temperaments.

Of course my father always agreed with my mother, that Saint Anthony saved the pair. Only he gave a different explanation of how the saint was effective.

'It was the light flashing on the case which blinded me that afternoon. So I turned back to see what it was.'

Uncle Titus always admired my father.

'He's a man who knows what he wants,' he would say to me every summer. 'You take a leaf out of his book, and you'll not do badly. He was always a man with plans.'

As a child I did not understand. I only knew that my mother was no sooner in the kitchen with my angry aunt, but the rows would begin. And that signified to me that the long school holidays had begun in earnest.

Deep Down

by Angela Bourke

I told Liam a story last night. His hand was on my stomach under my dress and I thought it might make him stop. It wasn't that I didn't like it. His hand was huge. I couldn't get over the size of it, but it was warm. The eyes were the same. Brown eyes that kept on looking at me after I thought he'd look away, so I started to tell him about this thing that happened hundreds of years ago, a story I often think about since I heard it. It's in a manuscript, but it happened not far from my own home – a place called Clonmacnois, on the Shannon. A lot of medieval things happened there.

It was in a church, with a whole crowd of people and a priest saying mass, just after the consecration, and the people heard a terrible racket, like something dragging along the roof. They all ran out and looked up, and there was a boat up there in the sky. An ordinary boat, like you'd see on the sea, or on a lake, but it was up above the roof of the church, just hanging in the sky. They were looking at the bottom of it. The light is very clear in Clonmacnois, specially when the river floods.

The anchor was caught in the church door. It was on the end of a long rope coming down through the air, and it was caught in the door they had just come through. That's what the noise was.

There must have been a terrible commotion. You can imagine them all standing around in the cold with their red faces, looking up, but the next thing was a man with no clothes on, just some kind of cloth, came swimming down towards them from the boat to get the anchor loose. I have to hold my breath just thinking about it. I'd have been scared stiff.

Some of the men grabbed him and held onto him. He was fighting to get away, but then they had to let go of him. He said: 'You're drowning me,' and they could see they were, so they stood back and he flew away from them.

His own people dragged him into the boat up above, and off they went, away across the sky the way they had come.

I often wonder if any ancestors of mine were there. They all went back into the church, and the priest finished mass. They always have to, I believe. It must have been hard for them, coming out at the end, not knowing if the world had changed, or only them. Liam gave me his jacket getting out of the car because the wind was chilly after the dance-hall. It came down to my knees, but it kept me warm. I never knew a leather jacket was so heavy. He made me take off my shoes as well, so I wouldn't ruin them on the beach. But what in the name of God was I doing there? What possessed me?

I'd no idea who he was at the beginning. I don't think I did. Anyone would have noticed him, the way he danced – like a ballet dancer. He reminded me of West Side Story, the tight jeans and the leather jacket – or your man Baryshnikov, the way the hair was flopping onto his forehead. He was taller than the rest of them as well. Longer legs.

A lot of the men around here are good dancers, but they're more heavy set – their centre of gravity is more in the seat of their trousers. I like dancing with them. I love it when they swing me off the ground and I just go with it, so my feet don't miss a beat when I hit the floor again. I like their strong wrists and the way they laugh a lot. But I don't think I'd ever lust after them.

I remembered some of them last night, from when I used to come and stay with Gracie. Men I used to think were old were only five or six years older than me – but then I was only about nineteen. They haven't changed much. Not compared with the women. I got a real shock when I saw some of them – girls that used to be beautiful. Now they're fat and half their teeth are gone and their hair is grey.

It always did me good to come here, I'm ashamed to say. I don't mean the sea air. That'd do anyone good, all the walking – but the dances, and people fancying me. A suitcase of clean clothes and my hair washed, and off I'd go. I thought I was so glamorous.

Of course at home there were never that many people around. The farms are bigger. I used to feel like an awkward big lump beside the town girls – half asleep and nothing to say, the way you'd see a caterpillar chewing its way through a cabbage leaf. But then I'd come down here and I'd turn into a butterfly, and that's what I was looking for this time too, never mind what I told Eamonn. I was starting to feel like a fat green lump again. That's not a good sign when you're walking around with fifteen hundred pounds worth of diamond engagement ring on your finger.

Liam doesn't know about Eamonn. The ring is back at home where I left it, in the drawer with my Irish dancing medals, and the subject never came up. He didn't even ask me where I was living now. It would have sounded foolish, at that hour of night. There was so much noise in the hall anyway. Nobody was talking. It's the old fashioned sort of place. The men all stay on one side and the women are all along the other. They have to walk across the floor to ask you to dance, and there's no such thing as saying no either, unless the man is really footless. When Liam came along he just reached between two other girls and took hold of my hand, and I just followed him.

His hand was warm, holding onto mine between sets. Dry. He was smiling over my head at the band, but he didn't say anything for ages.

I said nothing either, and now I wonder am I mad? I hardly said a word all evening, to tell the truth, until that time we got back into the car, but that's no excuse.

He did all the talking.

Such a memory! But I should have known better. God almighty – is he even twenty-one?

'Are you Linda Reilly?' he asked me at the end of the third set.

You could have knocked me down.

'Yes,' I said. But how did he know? He was young and gorgeous, towering over me, holding my hand. You'd think he had to look after me.

'You used to be my babysitter.' His teeth were perfect too.

'Oh my God!' It was like opening one of those dolls and finding another one inside. I knew what it was. 'Don't tell me. – You're not one of the Dunnes?'

'Liam,' he said, grinning all over his face. 'I knew you the minute I saw you. You came to stay with Gracie Ryan. You minded us when our mother went to hospital.'

I used to take them to the beach. Or they used to take me. The same beach we were on last night. Three of them. Liam was the eldest. All the Dunnes were blond, but he was the only one with brown eyes. He used to follow me around. He'd stay sitting with me when the other two were off having adventures. I thought he was worried about his mother.

'I used to dream about you,' he said with his arm around me, sitting on the same big rock, after he kissed me the first time. 'Did you know that? I was only nine, but I used to go to sleep all excited, thinking about my lovely babysitter.'

That smile again. Nobody around here has teeth that good. I could even see them in the dark.

'I couldn't believe it when I walked in there tonight and saw you. You haven't changed a bit, you know.'

I nearly choked when he said that, looking at the size of him.

'- You have,' I said, and we laughed ourselves silly at that. The rock was cold under us, but the sky was warm. And we had his jacket.

All the things you hear about strange men.

Babysitting is different. If kids like you, you feel all strong looking after them. And the funny thing is you feel safe – even after they grow up over six feet and hold your face in their two hands with their two thumbs on the edges of your mouth and their tongue kissing deep into it.

The only thing I worried about was corrupting him, and that made me laugh all over again as soon as I thought of it. I wasn't teaching Liam Dunne anything he didn't know already.

He was the one that started it. He was the one who said it was too cold for me, we should go back to the car.

Something stopped me all the same, in the car. I wasn't cold any more and with his hand on my stomach my whole body felt like some creamy liquid you could pour out of a jug, but then someone's headlights went across the sky. Everyone knows everyone else's cars around here. When it's dark you can feel you're the only people for miles, but you never are. Liam's mouth was up against my ear and I could feel his hot whispering, 'Trust me,' he said, 'I'll take care of you. It'll be all right. Just trust me.'

I could suddenly see myself in front of a whole crowd of people, holding onto the jug with the last drops dripping out. I could already feel the relief of warm skin after all the hard denim and zips, but I made him stop.

'My mother would love to see you again,' Liam said. Maybe that was it. He was sure she'd be delighted, but I could imagine the long cold look she'd give me, the questions about what I'm doing now, am I married yet? Oh, engaged? And what does he do? And where's your ring? Another long hard look, with Liam looking hurt and young, his face up near the low ceiling, not understanding.

I opened the window on my side to let the sound of the waves in. The wind came clean and salty, cooling our skin. That was when I told him about the boat in Clonmacnois.

'I was never there,' he said, tucking his shirt in,' but I heard about it. All the monks. It was a big city, I believe.'

'Was it?' I said, 'I didn't know that.'

'And you living beside it?' He sat back in his seat and took a packet of sweets out of somewhere, the way Eamonn would reach for his cigarettes.

'We had a teacher at the Tech that told us about it. I used to love all them stories. I never heard that one before though.'

'Could we go now, do you think?' I asked him. It was nearly three in the morning. He turned the key to start the engine, and I wound up my window,'

'You mightn't believe what I'm going to tell you,' he said, coming up over the rise past the first houses. His voice was grim, 'but something like that happened my grandfather back out there.'

'Out where?'

'In the bay there, a bit off the head.'

I sucked on my sweet. He must eat them all the time. They tasted like his kisses.

'He was out there with three other fellows, fishing for cod. They're all dead now. The last of them went Christmas last year.'

I waited, looking at the small haystacks and the fuchsia hedges appearing and disappearing in front of us when the headlights hit them.

'One of the other fellows was at the helm, and my granda had a line out. He felt a heavy sort of weight, and when he pulled it in, what do you think was on it?'

'What?'

'A baby.'

I felt an awful lurching. The sweet was in my mouth, but I didn't know what it was doing there. Why was he telling me this? And on a line? Hooked. A baby on a hook – not even in a net.

When I was about fifteen someone buried a dead baby in the corner of a field near us. Nobody let on they knew anything about it. The guards came around all the houses, but the girl was already gone to England.

I opened the window and Liam looked around at me, 'It wasn't dead,' he said quickly. He put his hand on my knee. Warm again.

'– That's what I'm telling you. It was a live baby, fit and well, with clothes on it.'

'How could it be alive?' I laughed with relief.

'That's what I don't know. All I know is my grandfather was one of the best fishermen around here, and he wasn't making it up.'

'They don't fish here any more do they?'

'Not since 1968.'

'Is that when the drownings were?'

'Two boatloads of men in one night. My granda was one of them.'

Liam was stopping the car. My guesthouse was in on our left, but I wanted to hear more.

'I didn't know that. You must have only been a baby then.'

'I wasn't even born. My mother was carrying me. I have all his things above in the house. She kept them for me. I'm called after him.'

'Did she tell you the story too?'

'She did. And she made me promise I'd never go fishing for a living.'

'It's a dangerous life all right.'

'There was another bit to the story too,' he said slowly, 'only it wasn't from my mother I heard it.'

'What was that?' I felt like his babysitter again. Careful. Maybe it was the houses around, or the paved road.

'One of the other old fellows that was out that day used to say they had to throw the child back.'

'Back into the water?' Funny I never even asked him what they did with it.

The car was very quiet with the engine off. I could see Liam's face in the light from the sky. He was looking straight ahead, leaning on the steering wheel, not touching me.

'I don't know,' he said quickly, 'but that's what they did. He said a woman came up beside the boat in the water and cursed them up and down for hooking the child out of its cradle down below.'

I didn't laugh. He wasn't laughing. I saw his hand go to the key and come back. His mother was on her own in the house, I suppose. He told me his two brothers were in Boston, and I knew his father was dead years ago. She'd probably lie awake till she heard the car.

'I'll go in,' I said. 'Thanks for the lift.'

He started the engine. The lights flashed a screen of stone wall and fuchsia hedge up in front of us.

'Sure I might see you tomorrow.' A bit of a smile at last.

'Sure you might, I suppose,' I said, smiling back. This was the usual chat, visitors flirting with locals. Harmless really.

I walked up to the front door, but I didn't go in. I stood there on my own in the quiet night, watching the car lights cut through the dark sky, listening to the sound of the engine until I couldn't hear it any more.

Luck be a Lady

by Anne Enright

The bingo coach (VZE 26) stopped at the top of the road and Mrs Maguire (no 18), Mrs Power (no 9) and Mrs Hanratty (no 27) climbed on board and took their places with the 33 other women and 0 men who made up the Tuesday run.

'If nothing happens tonight ... ' said Mrs Maguire and the way she looked at Mrs Hanratty made it seem like a question.

'I am crucified,' said Mrs Hanratty, 'by these shoes. I'll never buy plastic again.'

'You didn't,' said Mrs Power, wiping the window with unconcern.

'I know,' said Mrs Hanratty. 'There's something astray in my head. I wouldn't let the kids do it.'

Nothing in her tone of voice betrayed the fact that Mrs Hanratty knew she was the most unpopular woman in the coach. She twisted 1 foot precisely and ground her cigarette into the plastic mica floor.

When Mrs Hanratty was 7 and called Maeve, she had thrown her Clarks solid leather, solid heeled, T-bar straps under a moving car and they had survived intact. The completion of this act of rebellion took place at the age of 55, with a fake patent and a heel that made her varicose veins run blue. They pulsed at the back of her knee, disappeared into the fat of her thigh, ebbed past her caesarian scars and trickled into her hardening heart, that sat forgotten behind two large breasts, each the size of her head. She still had beautiful feet.

She kept herself well. Her silver hair was thin and stiff with invisible curlers and there was *diamante* in her ears. She was the kind of woman who squeezed into fitting rooms with her daughters, to persuade them to buy the cream skirt, even though it would stain. She made her husband laugh once a day, on principle, and her sons were either virgins or had the excuse of a good job.

Maeve Hanratty was generous, modest and witty. Her children succeeded and failed in unassuming proportions and she took the occasional drink. She was an enjoyable woman who regretted the fact that the neighbours (except perhaps, Mrs Power) disliked her so much. 'It will pass,' she said to her husband. 'With a bit of luck, my luck will run out.'

At the age of 54 she had achieved fame in a 5-minute interview on the radio when she tried to dismiss the rumour that she was the luckiest woman in Dublin. 'You'll get me banned from the hall,' she said.

'And is it just the bingo?'

'Just the bingo.'

'No horses?'

'My father did the horses,' she said, 'I wouldn't touch them.'

'And tell me, do you always know?'

'Sure, how could I know?' she lied – and diverted 126,578 people's attention with the 3 liquidisers, 14 coal-scuttles, 7 weekends away, 6,725 paper pounds, and 111 teddy-bears that she had won in the last 4 years.

'If you ever want a teddy-bear!'

'Maeve ... ' she said, as she put down the phone. 'Oh Maeve.' Mrs Power had run across over the road in her dressing-gown and was knocking on the kitchen door and waving through the glass. There was nothing in her face to say that Mrs (Maeve) Hanratty had made a fool of herself, that she had exposed her illness to the world. Somehow no one seemed surprised that she had numbered and remembered all those lovely things. She was supposed to count her blessings.

There were other statistics she could have used, not out of anger, but because she was so ashamed. She could have said 'Do you know something – I have had sexual intercourse 1,332 times in my life. Is that a lot? 65% of the occasions took place in the first 8 years of my marriage, and I was pregnant for 48 months out of those 96. Is that a lot? I have been married for 33 years and a bit, that's 12,140 days, which means an average of once a day every 9.09 days. I stopped at 1,332 for no reason except that I am scared beyond reason of the number 1,333. Perhaps this is sad.' It was not, of course, the kind of thing she told anyone, not even her priest, although she felt a slight sin in all that counting. Mrs Hanratty knew how many seconds she had been alive. That was why she was lucky with numbers.

It was not that they had a colour or a smell, but numbers had a feel like people had when you sense them in a room. Mrs Hanratty thought that if she had been in Auschwitz she would have known who would survive and who would die just by looking at their forearms. It was a gift that hurt and she tried to stop winning teddy-bears, but things kept on adding up too well and she was driven out of the house in a sweat to the monotonous comfort of the bingo call and another bloody coal-scuttle.

She was the 11th out of the coach, which was nice. The car parked in front had 779 on its number plate. It was going to be a big night.

She played Patience when she was agitated and on Monday afternoons, even if she was not. She wouldn't touch the Tarot. The cards held the memory of wet days by the sea, with sand trapped in the cracks of the table that made them hiss and slide as she laid them down. Their holiday house was an old double-decker bus washed up on the edge of the beach with a concrete block where the wheels should have been and a gas stove waiting to blow up by the driver's seat. They were numberless days with clouds drifting one into the other and a million waves dying on the beach. The children hid in the sea all day or played in the ferns and Jim came up from Dublin for the weekend.

'This is being happy, 'she thought, scattering the contents of the night bucket over the scutch grass or trekking to the shop. She started counting the waves in order to get to sleep.

She knew before she realised it. She knew without visitation, without a slant of light cutting into the sea. There was no awakening, no manifestation, no pause in the angle of the stairs. There may have been a smile as she took the clothes pegs out of her mouth and the wind blew the washing towards her, but it was forgotten before it happened. She just played Patience all day on the fold-down table in a derelict bus and watched the cards make sense.

By the age of 55 she had left the cards behind. She found them obvious and untrustworthy – they tried to tell you too much and in the wrong way. The Jack of Spades sat on the Queen of Hearts, the Clubs hammered away in a row. Work, love, money, pain; clubs, hearts, diamonds, spades, all making promises too big to keep. The way numbers spoke to her was much more bewildering and ordinary. Even the bingo didn't excite or let her down, it soothed her. It let her know in advance.

> 5 roses; the same as
> 5 handshakes at a railway station: the same as
> 5 women turning to look when a bottle of milk
>   smashes in the shop: the same as
> 5 odd socks in the basket
> 5 tomatoes on the window-sill
> 5 times she goes to the toilet before she can get to
>   sleep.
> and all different from

4 roses, 4 shakes of the hand, 4 women turning, 4 children, 4 odd socks, 4 tomatoes in the sun, 4 times she goes to the toilet and lies awake thinking about the 5th.

The numbers rushed by her in strings and verification came before the end of any given day. They had a party all around her, talking, splitting, reproducing, sitting by themselves in a corner of the room. She smoked them, she hung them out on the line to dry, they chattered to her out of the TV. They drummed on the table-top and laughed in their intimate, syncopated way. They were music.

She told no one and did the cards for people if they asked. It was very accurate if she was loose enough on the day, but her husband didn't like it. He didn't like the bingo either and who could blame him?

'When's it going to stop?' he would say, or 'the money's fine, I don't mind the money.'

'With a bit of luck,' she said, 'my luck will run out.'

On Wednesday nights she went with Mrs Power to the local pub, because there was no bingo. They sat in the upstairs lounge where the regulars went, away from the people who were too young to be there at all. Mr Finn took the corner stool, Mr Byrne was centre forward. In the right-hand corner Mr Slevin sat and gave his commentary on the football match which was being played out in his head. The other women sat in their places around the walls. No one let on to be drunk. Pat the barman knew their orders and which team were going to get to the final. At the end bar, Pauline made a quiet disgrace of herself, out on her own and chatty.

'His days are numbered ... ' said a voice at the bar, and Mrs Hanratty listened to her blood quicken. 'That fella's days are *numbered*.' There was a middle-aged man standing to order like a returned Yank in a shabby suit with a fat wallet. He was drunk and proud of it.

'I've seen his kind before,' he counted out the change in his pocket carefully in 10s and 2s and 5s, and the barman scooped all the coins into one mess and scattered them into the till. Mrs Hanratty took more than her usual sip of vodka and orange.

'None of us, of course,' he commented, though the barman had moved to the other end of the counter, 'are exempt.'

It was 2 weeks before he made his way over to their table, parked his drink and would not sit until he was asked. 'I've been all over,' he told them. 'You name it, I've done it. All over,' and he started to sing something about Alaska. It had to be a lie.

'Canada,' he started. 'There's a town in the Rockies called Hope. Just like that. And a more miserable stretch of hamburger joints and shacks you've never seen. Lift your eyes 30 degrees and you have the dawn coming over the mountains and air so thin it makes you feel the world is full of ... well what? I was going to say "lovely ladies" but look at the two I have at my side.' She could feel Mrs Power's desire to leave as big and physical as a horse standing beside her on the carpet.

He rubbed his thigh with his hand, and, as if reminded slapped the tables with 3 extended fingers. There was no 4th. 'Look at that,' he said, and Mrs Power gave a small whinny. 'There should be a story there about how I lost it, but do you know something? It was the simplest thing in the County Meath where I was as a boy. The simplest thing. A dirty cut and it swelled so bad I was lucky I kept the hand. Isn't that a good one? I worked a combine harvester in the great plains of Iowa and you wouldn't believe the fights I got into as a young fella as far away as ... Singapore – believe *that* or not. But a dirty cut in the County Meath.' And he wrapped the 3 fingers around his glass and toasted them silently. That night, for the first time in her life, Maeve Hanratty lost count of the vodkas she drank.

She wanted him. It was as simple as that. A woman of 55, a woman with 5 children and 1 husband, who had had sexual intercourse 1,332 times in her life and was in possession of 14 coal-scuttles, wanted the 3-fingered man, because he had 3 fingers and not 4.

It was a commonplace sickness and one she did not indulge. Her daughter came in crying from the dance hall, her husband (and not her father) spent the bingo money on the horses. The house was full of torn betting slips and the stubs of old lipstick. Mrs Hanratty went to bingo and won and won and won.

Although she had done nothing, she said to him silently, 'Well it's your move now, I'm through with all that,' and for 3 weeks in a row he sat at the end of the bar and talked to Pauline, who laughed too much. 'If that's what he wants, he can have it,' said Mrs Hanratty, who believed in dignity, as well as numbers.

The numbers were letting her down. Her daily walk to the shops became a confusion of damaged registration plates, the digits swung sideways or strokes were lopped off. 6 became 0, 7 turned into 1. She added up what was left, 555, 666, 616, 707, 906, 888, the numbers for parting, for grief, for the beginning of grief, forgetting, for accidents and for the hate that comes from money.

On the next Wednesday night he was wide open and roaring. He talked about his luck, that had abandoned him one day in Ottawa when he promised everything to a widow in the timber trade. The whole bar listened and Mrs Hanratty felt their knowledge of her as keen as a son on drugs or the front of the house in a state. He went to the box of plastic plants and ransacked it for violets which were presented to her with a mock bow. How many were there? 3 perhaps, or 4 – but the bunch loosened out before her and all Mrs Hanratty could see were the purple plastic shapes and his smile.

She took to her bed with shame, while a zillion a trillion a billion a million numbers opened up before her and wouldn't be pinned down at 6 or 7 or 8. She felt how fragile the world was with so much in it and confined herself to Primes, that were out on their own except for 1.

'The great thing about bingo is that no one loses,' Mrs Power had told him about their Tuesday and Thursday nights. Mrs Hanratty felt flayed in the corner, listening to him and his pride. Her luck was leaking into the seat as he invited himself along, to keep himself away from the drink, he said. He had nothing else to do.

The number of the coach was NIE 133. Mrs Maguire, Mrs Power and Mrs Hanratty climbed on board and took their places with the 33 women and 1 man who made up this Thursday run. He sat at the back and shouted for them to come and join him, and there was hooting from the gang at the front. He came up the aisle instead and fell into the seat beside Mrs Hanratty with a bend in the road. She was squeezed over double, paddling her hand on the floor in search of 1 ear-ring which she may have lost before she got on at all.

He crossed his arms with great ceremony, and not even the violence with which the coach turned corners could convince Mrs Hanratty that he was not rubbing her hand, strangely, with his 3 fingers, around and around.

'I am a 55-year-old woman who has had sex 1,332 times in my life and I am being molested by a man I should never have spoken to in the first place.' The action of his hand was polite and undemanding and Mrs Hanratty resented beyond anger the assurance of its tone.

All the numbers were broken off the car parked outside the hall, except 0, which was fine – it was the only 1 she knew anymore. Mrs Hanratty felt the justice of it, though it made her feel so lonely. She had betrayed her own mind and her friends were strange to her. Her luck was gone.

The 3-fingered man was last out of the coach and he called her back. 'I have your ear-ring! Maeve!' She listened. She let the others walk through. She turned.

His face was a jumble of numbers as he brought his hand up in mock salute. Out of the mess she took: his 3 fingers; the 3 of his eyebrows, which was laughing; the 3 of his upper lip and the 1 of his mouth, which opened into O as he spoke.

'You thought you'd lost it!' and he dropped the *diamante* into her hand.

'I thought I had.'

He smiled and the numbers of his face scattered and disappeared. His laughter multiplied out around her like a net.

'So what are you going to win tonight then?'

'Nothing. You.'

'O'

Midland Jihad

by Liz McManus

You don't forget the first time. After the first time you remember sensations, the excitement, the thrill of conquest. Even the fear you remember. But you don't separate one from the next. Things run together; hair on a forearm; the sparkle in an eye; blood. Yes, but whose hair? Whose eye? Sometimes I lie awake counting up the number I've had. Ten in seven years. Or is it eight in six? Either way it is not a bad record for a man only getting into his prime. I am thirty years old. The day I turned thirty I was holed up in West Mayo with a farmer. Some farmer he was. Sixteen acres of shit land and a car as big as a hearse. He had a sister with an evil tongue. She didn't want me in that house and she didn't rest until she got me out of it.

• • •

The first time; the sun climbing up the bright sky and me making my way through a field of grass. I felt big, like I was taking up more space in the world, even though I was humped down, so close to the ground that I could see ants creeping up the broken stalks. Our Father, I prayed, who art in Heaven. And heaven was near. Heaven was bundled up in the blue air above the fields. There were messages written for me in the air. When I stood up I felt full to bursting and high as a bird in the sky over Aughnacloy. I was ready to explode like a rocket. I was Tarzan. Uhuhuhuhuhu! that sound throbbing in my ears. It was great, I remember, my first time.

• • •

I don't remember Maggie Farrell. Maggie Farrell was a mistake.

• • •

After Mayo there was Mullingar. Wide wet streets, warm pubs and a church as big as a prison. Mullingar was a widow woman, she was soft in the head and unable to talk. She thought I was her son and she kept me for weeks. She drank nothing but soup, for her teeth were gone, so I got to eat what the Meals on Wheels brought. I would have been on the pig's back only for the fact that Mullingar is full of treacherous hoors. They had the clamps on me so tight that I was like a eunuch in a harem. All around me was opportunity and not a chance of grabbing any. I am only thirty years old but the way they saw it I was over the hill. A liability.

• • •

Maggie Farrell was a mistake.

But things happen. How was I to know?

• • •

In Mullingar I dyed my hair and grew a beard. That helped for a while. Sitting around in the old widow's house with nothing to do all day I came up with ideas but no-one would listen to me. They gave me money, I had a safe house, I could have retired quietly and no-one would have been the wiser. Settled down there maybe, married some Mullingar heifer with big ankles and a miraculous medal. It wasn't home but it was Ireland. After the war there would be an amnesty. Then I could bring her back to Belfast to Mammy. Shit, I got myself thinking the way they wanted. They wanted to do nothing in Mullingar. No Active Service

Unit, no war, nothing. Just sit around in the corner Bar talking. Talk, talk, talk bullshit.

• • •

But things happen. How was I to know?

What was she doing there in the middle of the night? Little Maggie Farrell.

• • •

I remember my first time in Aughnacloy; the two of them standing out from the checkpoint enjoying the sunshine and looking at the hedges along the roadside. Theus a yellahamma, says one of them. Gis awver yur glawses. Talking about birds and barely able to speak the King's English, the pair of them. Awri' Mick, says the other and hands him his binocs. Mick! I thought they only called us Mick. Mick and Paddy and bleeding bastards. I got the two of them. It was in every newpaper. Those binocs just flew away.

• • •

Little Maggie Farrell. Didn't she get headlines and a photo of herself in her First Communion dress?

I don't remember.

• • •

After a while I couldn't take the pub talk no more. One mouth bigger and louder than the next. I gave one of them a box and he went down. A row started and the guards were called. I'd done nothing but it finished me with Mullingar. The Branch came around and started asking questions. They had a lot to ask about. Ten in seven years. Or was it eight in six? Aughnacloy, Maghera, Aghalane, Roslea ... I wasn't about to let the Branch succeed in doing what the Brits had failed to.

• • •

After that it got hard. Days sleeping rough, in bogholes and in ditches. I moved at night mostly, creeping through the countryside like a rat under a hedge. Such silent places, they made me afraid. I'm afraid of nothing and nothing is what I got. Nothing but black turf ridges, one after the other and bogland, naked as the moon. I was afraid I'd go mad, the way I kept travelling in the dark, without a soul to talk to. The loneliness! It made me think of Jesus in the desert. Forty days and forty nights. Why keep going? I could have given up, settled for Mullingar, kept the head down and led a quiet life. I could have forgotten the struggle, forgotten Belfast, and closed my mind to everything except the hour, the minute of existence. After all, I'm getting on. I'm over thirty years old. I lost track of time and I began to lose faith. Eli, Eli, I cried, lama sabacthani? But no answer emerged out of the voiceless dark.

• • •

Until the third day.

• • •

And even so, when that power station appeared up from the bog I remember thinking, this is it, I've gone fucking crazy. Out of the night it reared, a concrete cliff with bright lights and chimneys taller than Divis Flats. Funny the way it reminded me of Belfast and our flats. All that concrete and, inside, people working. Not that many I knew in our flats worked, but from the windows you can see across the city to the shipyards and the tall cranes where the Prods have the jobs. Home Sweet Home c/o The ESB power station. Rhode, County Offaly – the nearest to home I'm likely to get. After being out on the bog so long, that power station looked sweet to me. A fence ran along its perimeter and the gates were closed but I wasn't put off. There was a shed built up against the fence, with a roof on it to keep out the rain and a broken lock on the door. My legs ached. It was warm in the shed and through the cracks in the door came the glow from the arc lights of the power station. Signs of life. Here was the comfort I wanted after the empty miles I had walked, comfort enough to rest my head easy and I was grateful that God in His mercy had delivered me. Sufficient unto the day is the evil thereof, I thought before I drowned in sleep.

• • •

Later I woke up, muggy, trailing the tail-end of a dream. I dreamt that I was buried in a boghole. Water dripped around me; soft mould crumbled in my mouth. At first the sound I heard seemed to belong to my dream; the sound of breathing like someone running hard. I kept quiet in the corner. It could have been a night watchman, a security man, someone to blow the gaff and send me back out into the cold. The breathing slowed and then it rose into a wail like a cat's. It made my hair stand on end, that thin wail of fear. Then a girl's voice hissed, 'Who's that?'

I said nothing.

'Jesus!' she was up close staring into my face. 'The fright you gave me.'

She was only a kid. A kid with a dirty face. Her eyes scoured the dark.

'You a knacker?' she asked.

I told her I was just passing through and she smiled a ghost of a smile and said, join the club. I found myself wanting to talk to her. Loneliness can have that effect on you. In the Movement you get warned about it. The first friendly face you meet and you sing like a canary. But who could she tell my story to, a kid like that?

'I'm on the run.'

She giggled, 'Did the nuns throw you out?'

Her flippancy irritated me.

'Listen,' I said, 'I'm no knacker. I did time once and now there's men searching the country for me. I've come all the way from Mullingar.'

Silence.

'On business, wee girl. I have important business to do.' The words just flowed. I couldn't stop them.

'What kind of business?'

As if I'd tell her. Cheeky brat. A wain like her, what was she doing hiding out in a shed in the middle of the night?

'Never you mind,' I said.

She looked away as if she didn't really care one way or the other. Now I was pursuing her.

'Have you no home to go to?'

She didn't answer. Her head turned towards me again, full into the narrow band of light. She didn't look like much, her face bloated and wet with sweat. She looked sick and her sickness infected the air. Sickness and fear and the stink of the lavatory bowl. All around me I could smell her fear. Her mouth opened. 'What is it?' I asked.

She panted like a dog, her eyes bulging, her skinny arms pulling at her anorak. 'What is it?'

Again I heard that animal wail as her body distended and the anorak dropped onto the ground. A tee-shirt stretched across her swollen paunch and God revealed her shame to me. Her abdomen quivered and her little sticks of arms swept the darkness. I was reminded of ants on a gob of cuckoo-spit shaking a reed of grass.

'Our Father who are in Heaven,'

The blue sky over Aughnacloy and the world poised to explode.

'Hallowed be Thy Name.'

She laughed at the sound of my words. I stopped but her hand found refuge in mine.

'Keep praying,' she said, 'I need all the help I can get.'

• • •

Thy Kingdom come. I prayed and the air was torn by a cry as bitter and ancient as the bog outside. Was it happening because of my prayer? Fear skinned along my spine. I let go her hand and knelt on the ground. Thy Will be done. Without guidance I eased her down and my fingers sought between her legs. She moaned quietly and I was glad of the night, dreamy and dark and all-encompassing.

• • •

We both waited for the tide to rise again. When I felt it coming, heard it in her voice as she cried out I knew that I could carry her voice with mine. I had the strength. Deliver us from evil ... I called, loud and certain above the strips of pain issuing from her mouth. Deliver us ... Our voices rose together. At last, satisfied to be finished, she sank and, with no more than a whisper of regret, released her prize. Out gushed the living stream into my waiting hands, its wet bundle slithering between my fingers.

• • •

I don't remember. I remember. The Word made Flesh.

• • •

She said nothing after, not one word. She just buried her head in her arms and curled up on the ground. Her skin was white as a corpse. Even when the sound of the baby's cries filled the shed she didn't budge. My way was clear. I never saw her again after, except for the smudged photograph with its black border in the newspaper. I wrapped her anorak around the baby. It was, of course, a boy.

• • •

Outside the sky had brightened. The lights of the power station were waning as day built up in the east. After the long darkness there was dew in the air. Birds drifted out of the trees. Somewhere women stood in kitchens, filling up kettles, boiling eggs, wiping sleep from their faces.

• • •

There is only one street in Rhode, one street and one church at the end of it. One Holy Catholic and Apostolic Church. In my despair I had sought a sign and at the darkest hour of night I had been rewarded in abundance. The doors of the church were locked. I laid the baby on the step and tucked the anorak around him. Above his head the air was still, its warmth touching the edges of morning. He looked so tranquil there, so much at peace after his journey. Yet, even in sleep, his tiny fists were clenched.

• • •

I would go on.

• • •

For Thine is the Power, Thine is the Power, Thine is the Power and the Glory.

The Lift Home

by Mary Dorcey

He was meticulous and considerate. He always spread a clean, white, linen handkerchief over his lap before they started. She wondered who washed them. Was it a maid or his wife? Would she put them in with everything else? Or boil them separately? They were always immaculate anyhow. When they were finished he refolded the handkerchief in four, straightened his clothes and tidied himself away with the same precise businesslike air with which he returned his fountain pen, after signing a cheque, to his inside pocket.

He had been driving her home for more than three months now, all through the dark wet nights of winter. Dropping her off on the corner of Firbank Road, two streets down from her own. Lending her his umbrella to keep her hair dry if it was raining. Though she hardly noticed the weather anymore. In the smooth, dark blue Vauxhall with the radio on and the heater going full blast they were impervious to the outside world.

It had started by accident. In the old days before they came to their arrangement she was never sure how she would manage for a lift home. She could go with Paulo the chef if he was in the mood or get a lift with old Brian the doorman, but that could mean hanging about until four in the morning. Then one night they were both off sick and she was stuck. She was waiting on the street for a taxi when Mr Conway offered to take her home. It was scarcely out of his way, he said. No trouble at all. She lived on the northside and so did he.

As it happened, it was more than five miles off his

route, she found out later. But it did not matter to him that night or any other, the extra time or the petrol. It was more than worth it to have the pleasure of a lady's company.

He was a gentleman. The first night he drove her straight to the door and wished her goodnight without so much as touching her knee. And again on the next. On the third he gave her a small kiss on the cheek. On the fourth day he bought her a box of dairy milk chocolates and said, 'something for the children,' as he handed it to her. It was on that night that he told her the story of his life. The gradual and all too commonplace descent into disillusion, as he put it. He talked in a strange, abstracted fashion about his own experience and feelings as though sharing a private joke with himself, but one that did not make him laugh. He was a senior Civil Servant with the Board of Works. She did not know what that meant. She had a mental image of a long wooden table with all kinds of articles laid out as for a sale of work. But he told her it had to do with land and national monuments. He had a very comfortable salary he assured her. Well above the requisite thirty pieces of silver. He told her about his family, his wife who was an invalid, at least in a manner of speaking, a diabetic who drank. He had long since abandoned the struggle to make her take care of herself. It was the children who suffered of course in such circumstances. For himself it scarcely mattered anymore. He was immune. Except that her illness had for many years made normal life impossible. Normal 'married' life that was to say. Normal for a man, if she understood what he meant. And she did. She knew only too well how unusual normal life was. How easily you could slip from its hold.

She had danced in the chorus line of the Gaiety theatre. For almost nine years a 'Gaiety Girl'. She still had the legs to prove it. She could still manage the old routine almost as well as ever. In the club sometimes in the early part of the evening before the customers came in she would go through the workout to amuse the rest of the staff, holding onto the counter while she kicked her legs high. Go on, they would call, applauding, clapping their hands in rhythm. It was a matter of pride to her to be able to carry it off nearly as well as she had in her heyday. Her days of glory as the others called it.

Mr Conway had never seen her performance of course, because he never came in until after eleven. And he had never made any remark on her legs. He was not a 'legs man', it was her hair he admired; her blonde curls (helped out by the bottle now) that reached to her shoulder, her bright blue eyes, and the upper half of her body; her womanly figure, as he phrased it. Before and afterwards sitting in the darkness of the parked car he would press his head against her breast and request her to stroke his forehead. Sometimes at these moments he murmured a few words. Once he had cried.

He had been coming in for almost six months before he offered her the lift home. Twice a week, Tuesdays and Thursdays, always before midnight. You could set your watch by him. He sat without fail at the corner table and ordered fillet steak or chicken Kiev. Mr Conway at table ten asking for you, the others would say and she would go down to bring him his champagne. As soon as it was open he offered her the first glass. She appreciated that. Others drinking brandy themselves all night never sent up more than a house red for the staff. Generous and good mannered he was. You could tell that at once. And lonely. He had a face like a priest, she thought, stern and high principled because of the pale narrow cheekbones or the downward cast of his mouth? He looked out of place in that setting – the romantic music, the candlelight, the red table-cloths. Not that there was any reason a respectable man should not have come in for a drink, a quiet meal and maybe a couple of dances if one of the younger girls would oblige. Some even brought their wives. It was that kind of place, the Paradiso. Old-fashioned. The first of its kind on the street. It attracted the more mature client who appreciated traditional ways – jacket and tie – no unaccompanied females, no drunks, or at least not at the singing or shouting stage. He had liked her to serve him from the first, he said, because of her graceful movements. Ah, training stands to you, he said when he heard about her career in the theatre.

Well, her dancing days were done. Her days in the limelight. She was a deserted wife now with three small children to feed. It was surprising how much they had in common, Mr Conway said once, when you considered it. Both of them married in name only. Both of them raising offspring more or less single-handed. Except that his were next to grown up whereas hers were all under ten. He knew that it caused her anxiety to leave young children at night even though their granny came in after ten. But it was better she considered and he agreed with her, to have it that way than to have them on their own in the day time with no one to bring them to school or collect them after it, to leave them to get their own dinner or tea. Besides, she said, once they were asleep how could they miss her? He said a mother could worry too much. He said boys grew out of asthma and school reports meant nothing at that age. He said it to comfort her. He had always been nice about the kids.

After the first night it became a set understanding between them. 'Your coach is waiting, Madame,' Mrs. O', the manageress would say with a wink when at five past two Mr Conway brought the car around. He opened the door for her and settled her in, advising her always to fasten her seat-belt. It meant the world to her to be sure of the lift, to know exactly at what hour she would be home. It meant she could plan her day; organise herself properly for the first time. It meant she could be in bed as early as three o'clock some nights. And be up before the kids in the morning. Not waking to find them, as she used to, calling her from the kitchen. Or having her youngest, Sandra, stagger up the stairs with a cup of coffee to coax her from sleep. And so it continued for several weeks in that fashion, Tuesdays and Thursdays driven straight to her door. Nothing more to it than the bit of a chat and a kiss or two.

When one night in the week before Christmas he had wanted to prolong their conversation he had taken thought to stop the car short of her street, just before the Castle Court Hotel and park it close to the curb, well in under the shadow of the trees that overhung the railings. Near enough to the car-park to benefit from the flow of traffic and the presence of other stationary cars so that they were in no sense conspicuous to a passer-by. He had more drink taken that evening perhaps than was customary. The festive spirit as he said. And so had she. She tried to stick to white wine, but you had to take whatever was sent up. He put his suggestion more than politely. He reminded her once more of how lonely he was. The abnormal situation that would place a burden on any man. Any man of normal temperament. A small service was all he required. A service for which he would be most appreciative. And grateful if she took his meaning. She did. There was no need to spell anything out. Although coming from a man of his reserve it did not surprise her. It seemed to follow quite naturally from his kindness to her, the lift home, the box of chocolates, the kiss on the cheek. Afterwards that evening he had slipped a folded bank note into her bag and when she complained he insisted. Something for the children, he said again. When she got in, she found it was a ten pound note he had given her. She could hardly credit it. Twice a week, for half an hour. It was as much as she earned in one night at the club. It meant she could make a start next week on the telephone bill and buy Jason the new football boots.

It had started with ten pounds and now it was twelve, though she did not do anything more than she had at the beginning. Except that the time they spent in conversation grew longer. And it was conversation that he really needed. The opportunity to express himself freely. Air the small day-to-day troubles and frustrations. To tell her, because he had no one else to tell, his wife being long past rational discourse. That was why he came, after all. Why he had offered her a lift home in the first place. A sympathetic ear, as he had said the first night. A shoulder to cry on, smiling his grave sad smile.

It took a while to get used to, of course. To get over any awkwardness. The first time as soon as she got in she went straight up to the bathroom and washed her face and her hands and rinsed her mouth. But very soon she found she adapted. She learned to switch off her mind immediately as easily as a tap. Or to let it concern itself with practical details; the timetable for the week or what to wear for the parent and teachers meeting. She could afford, for the first time, to buy something nice. It surprised her to find that she sometimes felt proud. She felt she was helping him to bear a strain that might have been intolerable otherwise. She told herself that for all she knew she might be helping his family. He needed a certain service and she performed it. She did it as well as she knew how. To please him. And to justify the generosity of the money he gave her.

In some respects it was easier than it had been with her husband. Not that she was not in love with Gerry in the early days before the drinking began. In fact, they had been mad for one another in the first few years. And maybe that was why. Sometimes even now, looking back on things they had done and said in the height of passion, she could feel herself blush. Just because of the pleasure she had taken in it. Because sometimes she had asked for something she wanted to satisfy herself. And afterwards she would not know if he had done it just to please her or himself. Even though they were married and in the privacy of their own four walls there would be a residue of guilt and embarrassment. It was like helping yourself to the last piece of cake on a plate. You took it but you were uneasy as soon as you had it finished.

With Mr Conway it was quite straightforward. He kept his eyes shut the whole time and sat almost without stirring except to run his fingers through her hair, playing with it, grasping it, at the end, in both hands. So that she needed to comb it before going into the house. Once he had knocked her face against the steering wheel by accident and given her a black eye. The next evening he had brought her a bouquet of twelve red roses. He had kept them on the back seat of the car so as not to cause attention and presented them only when they were well past the club.

Well, and how have you been keeping? he would ask as soon as she got into the car. She liked that about him. Reliable and good mannered. Not too bad thanks, she would reply, all things considered. The journey home had fallen into an easy rhythm. They had their set ways and topics of conversation. For the most part he talked and she listened. But every so often a way she had of phrasing things would put something in perspective, shed new light on it. You're a very unusual woman he would say at such times. Driving home through the quiet empty streets in the small hours, she enjoyed their talk, with the steady purr of the engine, the radio playing night music, the warmth of the heater on her legs that were tired from hours of walking between tables. She liked to hear stories from another side of life. It was a comfort to know that even those with all the material blessings had their troubles.

She supposed in a manner of speaking you could say they were friends. That was what the other girls all called him – your friend Mr Conway. And that was why when spring came, the month of May, and with it the season of the First Holy Communions, it was he she thought of first. Or at least it was Molly, the head waitress at the club, who had made the suggestion. They were in the ladies at ten to two on a Tuesday night. She was making up her face, re-applying rouge and lipstick to be fresh for the journey home. She was telling Molly that her youngest, Sandra, was making her Communion on the twenty-fifth, in three weeks time, and she had not the half of it bought yet. There was nothing you could tell Molly about Communions. She had put three of her own through it in four years. Not to mention the Confirmation. Every year was worse than the last they agreed. Every year it seemed to descend without warning just when you thought you were straight after the Christmas and Easter. In fact she was better off this year than any other, thanks to Mr Conway. But she did not say that to Molly. She told her the problem was the nuns who wanted to make a video of it. Which meant everyone would have to look as though they had stepped out of a fashion plate. Molly knew exactly. There was no one like the nuns for extravagance. But sure how could they know any better. How much did she need anyway? Well the thing was she had chipped a front tooth last summer. She would have to get it fixed if she was going to be on camera. It would set her back the best part of thirty pounds. Not to mention everything else she had to get. Why don't you ask your friend, Mr Conway? Molly said. He seems generous enough. I'm sure he'd give you the loan of a few bob if you asked him nicely. No, she had a dread of borrowing, she said. She wouldn't go into debt, whatever happened. She had seen too many go down that road.

Even the smallest loan could set you on the slippery slope. Well, he's the only one we know who'd have it, Molly said. And she called over her shoulder as she went out the door – Think about it!

And she did. For the next few days she thought about very little else. Every night after that on the journey home as they went through their usual topics she was abstracted, only half listening because she was debating in her mind whether or not to raise the subject. Wondering if there was any way she could sound him out. She did not want to ask, however well off he was. She did not want to be under any obligation. She preferred to keep their affairs as they stood – all above board and impersonal. She remembered once he had shown her a photo of his own girl Clare on her Confirmation day outside the Church of Mary Immaculate. Standing, smiling up at her father – proud as punch. It was a lovely day, he said apart from the cut of her mother, like a drunken sailor with her make-up running. Surely that meant he would understand how important it was on these occasions to have everything right?

In her mind she divided the journey into quarters, though they were not of equal length. The first three were taken up with the subjects of the club, work and family. The last was the time they spent outside the Castle Court. They began always with the club. Had it been a good night or a slow one? Had he enjoyed his meal, the music? Had he got a dance at all? He knew all the waitresses by name; Anne, Molly, Liz and Julie and Barbara who played the records and entertained customers who came in alone. I can never tell those two apart, he would say, which was strange because they looked totally different. One so dark, the other blonde. She was particularly fond of them both. They were nice girls. A bit mad but nice. She liked to sit with them in the early part of the evening, listening to their jokes, sharing a drink and a cigarette. They were too young to be working those hours, Mr Conway said. And they couldn't need the money. Well she didn't know. One was a student and the other worked in a shoe shop. They did it for the laugh she supposed more than anything. The men were wild for them, but they kept their distance. She had seen a boyfriend with them the occasional time but nothing serious. They were an odd pair, Mr Conway considered, cavorting about on the dance floor, oblivious of everyone. And she agreed, they were unusual, always laughing, always together. Wouldn't you envy them though, she asked, having someone you could trust completely, someone you could say anything to? Ah well, they were young yet. They had it all before them.

When he turned onto the sea road it was time to talk of the office. He had a lot of aggravation with colleagues because as he said he wasn't a man to suffer fools gladly. Sycophants, he would say scornfully, duplicity, the nod and the wink. And once when she asked about his prospects he only smiled and said oh but we rise by crawling – wasn't it always thus in the uncivil service? The last two miles before the Castle Court were spent on his family. He liked to talk of his eldest boys, Robert and Peter, both at university both playing rugby for the college. And Clare, the brains of the family and the prettiest. It was the youngest, Paul, who gave cause for concern. Always in hot water. A spendthrift like his mother. And she would remind him then of Jason who suffered from asthma because nothing mattered so long as they had their health, wasn't that right? And he agreed with her. It was true, he supposed, if you thought of it. And very soon another evening was over and she still had said nothing.

On Thursday night, the last time she would see him before Saturday, he was late coming in. It had never happened before. For more than an hour she was in a panic that he would not come at all. Eventually he arrived in after midnight, but she was so busy by then she could not get down to him.

When he brought the car round at five past two it was raining. He drove through a puddle as she stood waiting and muddy water splattered her stockings. Her new stockings that she had put on especially. As soon as she got in beside him her heart fell. She saw at once he was in bad form. His long pale lips were drawn tight at the corners. He asked how was she keeping without looking up and did not notice that she was wearing her white satin blouse that he always admired. She would have to get him talking straight away, coax him out of it or she might as well forget the whole thing. She had made up her mind, two nights ago, to ask him. But not for a loan. She had thought of another way. She had decided on the exact phrase to use, the exact words that would express her meaning with no risk of misunderstanding or embarrassment. But each time her nerve had failed her at the last minute. If she did not say it tonight she would never say it.

She began with Mrs O', the manageress who was always good for a laugh – letting on to be a teetotaller when everyone knew she survived on the hip flask she kept under the counter. But he hardly smiled and made no comment. She tried all the usual subjects; the club, the office – anything strange or startling, but he refused to show any interest. As they turned onto the coast road she asked why he had been late in. We missed you, she said. But he only sighed and answered reluctantly, domestic concerns. It was his family, then, that was bothering him was it? She asked after each of them in turn with no success until she got to Paul. Ah, that was it. His face was paler than ever, almost grey. That wastrel, he said contemptuously. What had he done? she asked. Oh nothing at all – he's only been threatened with expulsion from the best school in the country. And for what? For a female! Some little floozy he picked up in a dance-hall! She said that was terrible, to soothe him, but he was at that age. Wouldn't he get sense? Perhaps, he said, but whether he does or not I wash my hands of him. And then she saw they had reached the Castle Court.

The rain had stopped. But fat slow drops fell from the wet trees overhead and ran down the roof and windows. He switched off the lights and the engine. But instead of removing his glasses and placing them carefully upright on the dashboard as he always did, he sat motionless staring ahead with a strange distant expression in his eyes. What was wrong with him? Was it only Paul he was worried about? Suddenly he turned to face her and asked abruptly after Michelle and Sandra. She was taken aback. He never asked personal questions at this stage. He was making her nervous and out of nerves she said stupidly: Did I tell you Sandra is making her Communion on Saturday? Ah! and he smiled for the first time. A lovely age, unspoilt. Make the most of it. Well it isn't easy as it once was, she replied. And the kids get that excited it would break your heart to disappoint them. She had not intended to say any of this yet. She had wanted to wait until the end of the evening when they had completed the whole procedure. But his sympathy and the relief of being able to talk about it after all the weeks of silent worry brought it spilling from her. Indeed they're right, he answered solemnly. It is a special day. A day to remember. Perhaps if she told him now ... perhaps this was her chance. If she itemised all the expenses because a man could have no idea how much was involved? Maybe she should admit that it was not just for Sandra she needed money? Would he think her vain and selfish? Would a man understand that a mother had to look well herself for her children's sake? Would he know how painful it was to see them grow up to be critical of you? After all the years of work and worry, so that they would want for nothing, to see them look at you with cold eyes. Embarrassed by you. Like the other day when she was trying on the suit she had had cleaned for the Communion and in walked Michelle and stared at her and said – You're not going to wear that old thing again are you? You look ancient in it! And that was what made her mind up. From that moment on she was determined. She would not have her own children looking down on her. Ashamed. Would he understand that?

You see ... she began hesitantly, it's not only the kids you have to buy for ... with the way things are in the schools now, it's nearly as important how the parents look ... O don't I know, he said scornfully. That's today's world for you. Turning it into a circus like everything else. When I was a boy we were happy with half-a-crown. Now they tell me they go from door to door and they're not satisfied until they've made twenty pounds! She sank back into her seat, dreading what she had unleashed. His voice continued clipped and precise: Videos, I hear are the latest gimmick ... if I had my way they would all wear their ordinary school uniforms. Put a stop to this exhibitionism. Of course, it's the mothers I blame ... togging them out like little mannequins. But then ... he paused and smiled grimly, what woman can resist the opportunity to squander money? He looked at her and shook his head as though more in sorrow than anger. But it's getting late, he added, I mustn't keep you, must I? and he took off his spectacles and let his seat into recline position.

He lit a cigarette and drew deeply from it. He was very economical about his smoking. He enjoyed it only at certain times of the day, he said, after dinner, at breakfast and such like. He offered one to her but she refused it. She had not yet given up hope of asking and she thought it would not look right to have a cigarette in her hand. He was talking about rugby, his voice relaxed and amiable again, about some try scored against Blackrock College last Saturday. Isn't that great, she said, though it meant nothing to her. Her attention was caught only by the oddity of the expression. If it was only a try what was the excitement about? And if it was proper score why was it called a try? In a moment, he would say, well time waits for no man. He would refold his handkerchief and start the motor. First he checked the side mirror always particular about procedure. His face was averted from her which made it easier.

I was wondering ... she began, I was wondering ... her heart was beating faster, her hand played with the beads of a necklace about her throat, I was wondering ... if there was anything else ... Her voice was calm and level and yet there was a new edge to it – an undertone of something else. Appeal was it? Flirtatiousness? ... yes that was it, she could hear herself flirting with him. Anything, she lowered her eyes and raised them again. She made herself smile. She thought of Sandra. Of how she wanted her to look the day after tomorrow, how she wanted to see her smiling up at her mother, proud of her. Is there anything else at all I could do for you? He looked shocked. He had not quite understood her but he had caught the change of tone alright. She was so practical normally that it startled him as much as if she had kissed him. How do you mean ... ? he asked as cautious as she was. It was her turn to gaze ahead through the rain flecked windscreen. As she did so, composing her next sentence, she noticed two young women standing under a street lamp at the entrance to the hotel car-park.

Under the garish white radiance of the light they stood like figures on a stage, isolated from the bleak darkness around them. They faced each other, looking intently into the other's eyes. One was dark, the other blonde. As she watched, the dark one reached out and laid a hand on the other's shoulder. They remained for a moment perfectly still. Like young lovers she thought, and smiled at the absurdity of the phrase. They wore bright fashionable clothes, short skirts and tightly fitting T-shirts. For an instant something about them struck her as familiar. What was it? – their clothes, their hair-style, their way of standing; the rapt concentration on one another? An odd pair she thought. And then it stuck her ... Julie and Barbara of course ... that was who it was! She should have known them at once ... You were asking if there was anything I might like ... Mr Conway's precise voice broke into her thoughts, did you mean by that ... she looked at him, his face was lowered but she saw that he still held the white handkerchief in his hand as though uncertain whether or not to return it to his pocket. Because ... if by any chance you mean by that ... he continued hesitantly, measuring his words with care. As he spoke. a sudden roar of anger came from the street. With a quick impulse of fear her eyes returned at once to the young women she had been watching. And she saw that they were standing now in one another's arms, embracing. And behind them, running past the parked cars, was a man in a black leather jacket shouting and waving something in the air. At the same moment the two girls saw him and with one glance over their shoulder they took to their heels, fleeing from him with an almost mechanical haste. The man followed after them, lurching clumsily from side to side, shouting louder still and waving what she could see now was an empty bottle above his head. The girls were running under the shadow of the trees towards the car where she was sitting. Do you see those two girls, she said to Mr Conway, running towards us ... Where? he asked and, nonchalantly began to wipe his spectacles with a corner of his handkerchief ... what girls? It's Julie and Barbara ... they're being chased by that man ... What? he said ... that pair ... here? ... at this hour? Nonsense! he put on his glasses.

The girls were almost level with them now, they came rushing forward hand-in-hand, the dark one almost hauling the other off her feet. It is, she said, I'm sure of it ... The man was still pursuing them but was too unsteady on his legs to make much progress. Mr Conway turned on the headlights. The girls staggered, blinded for a moment. She turned to open the door but in her agitation could not find the handle. The girls had reached them. They stumbled against the bonnet. She heard them giggle. Will you come on for Jasus sake ... one of them said to the other, wrenching at her, and they lurched forward once more. As they passed the window she saw them full in the car lights, starkly illuminated – their young faces lurid with make-up purple rouge and lipstick, their eyes blackened as though bruised with mascara and shadow. She had never before seen either of them in her life. What on earth had made her think she knew them? What had induced her to imagine they were Julie and Barbara? They were gone past now. The man's voice sounded from behind the car: I'll fuckin' murder you ... if I fucking ... And then he had passed by them also, lurching his way into the darkness.

'Will you not do something?' ... she beseeched Mr Conway. 'We can't leave them to that man ...'

'For goodness sake!' he said, 'what are you thinking of? What could I do?'

'But they might be mugged ... raped ... anything ...'

'Raped?' he repeated, incredulous. And then to her astonishment he broke into a harsh laugh, a vulgar laugh quite unlike him. 'Raped, those two?' he said, 'that'll be the day!'

'What do you mean?' she asked uneasily.

'For Heaven's sake,' he said, 'can you not see what they are? They're street walkers ... nothing more than common prostitutes! Believe me, you leave that kind to their own devices!'

She sat bewildered, staring blankly ahead into the now empty street. Then she added uncertainly, 'Even so ... we can't just sit here and leave them to be ...'

'For the love of God, woman,' he broke out exasperated, 'how can a whore be raped? Would you tell me that?'

The words seemed to strike her like a blow. She almost flinched. And yet they meant nothing to her. She could not grasp them. She repeated them in her mind, feeling dull and foolish. What was wrong with her? Why had she felt so concerned for them? He was right, she supposed. It never did any good to interfere.

Listen ... his voice was gentle again and polite, will I drive you the rest of the way ... just this once? It's not safe to have you walking alone with these kind of ruffians about? He started the engine and pulled out onto the street before she could answer. They drove the length of Firbank Avenue in silence. He turned into Parkgrove and a moment later into Grace Heights.

He stopped the car on the corner with the engine still running. She took a comb from her bag to tidy her hair. By the way ... what was it you were about to ask me earlier?

Oh ... nothing, she said, nothing that won't keep. She returned the comb to her bag and closed it. She heard herself remark in a forlorn wounded tone: They were only children, you know. Children? He exclaimed, and then he laughed again. Look, take it from me – their kind are born women!

She opened the door and stepped out. The cold wet night stung her face. Suddenly she wanted to be gone from him. She wanted to be alone with her daughters in her own home. Alone with this new feeling that had come over her. A bewildered, obscure sense of guilt. And shame.

Just a moment, he said, she felt him touch her elbow, haven't you forgotten something? Looking down she saw him holding out a crisp twenty pound note. They were always brand new notes he gave her. He must have got them especially. She used to think it a mark of his delicacy. She hesitated. Then took it from his hand. She found then that she was holding two notes, not one.

Something for the Communion, he said, smiling his grave, weary smile.

Hyacinths

by Clairr O'Connor

Kate's father, Frank, couldn't sleep. He was not tired enough and had had too little to drink. The full moon penetrated the thin bedroom curtains, lighting up his room, his misery.

Blast and damn Kate! Where had she hidden the whiskey this time? It wasn't in her wardrobe, her chest of drawers, old favourites. Neither was it in the scullery hidden behind the pots and pans. The scullery hideout lasted a long time. He'd never have discovered it being averse to cooking for himself only that Tom Sheehy had called last week after midnight and Frank, benign host and insomniac, had offered him a boiled egg and toast. And there in a covered pot in the scullery stood a golden bottle of Paddy.

A gift for the night demons, to hold their horror at bay. It had started in mid-August. The scratching and squeaking of mice, heard at first, when he woke in the middle of the night. Then seen; dozens, dancing on the oval rug on his floor. The rug with the greeting *Fáilte*. Finally, they moved up the duvet on his bed, peering straight at him. The following day he bought poison and mousetraps and set them all over the house. To no avail. They were waiting for him every night.

Awake, with nothing to drink, he pulled the bedclothes tentlike over himself to blank out the moon's light. He tensed himself for the first squeal. The ridiculous rhyme, 'Why do you hide the Paddy from your Daddy?' came to him and drummed itself on and on in his head. The mice squeaked in rhythm.

• • •

Mrs Moloney, Frank's housekeeper, was sitting comfortably beside the electric log fire in her room. She was thinking about Kate. That one had no morals. You couldn't count the times that Lambourne man had been up to her attic room. She was up to no good. Muttering to herself she was the other day. Something to do with hyacinths. Anyone would go daft if they spent all their time summer and winter moping in a garden. Not to talk about her gallivanting into Dublin every night of the week.

• • •

Something would have to be done about Frank, Kate thought as she munched her biscuits in the cubbyhole at Knightclean, grandly called the staff canteen. The room measuring ten foot square contained; one table, six chairs, a shelf for mugs, tea, coffee and an electric kettle. Mrs O'Shea from Ballymun, the only other person in the room, was easing her feet out of her shoes to let her corns breathe.

'But a person must keep cheerful,' she was saying, a phrase with which she summed up all news good or bad. Kate was not following the conversation. She continued her preoccupation with her father's problems while maintaining a nodding assent to Mrs O'Shea's monologue. He would have to be sent somewhere to dry out. How to get him to consent was the first problem and how to pay for it the second.

• • •

Frank woke with a start, the remnants of a dream clinging to him. Mouth parched, eyes dry and gritty. He moved his false teeth about. Only six o'clock in the morning. Kate wouldn't be back till eight. The silly bitch out night cleaning. It was enough to mortify a man and her with a degree in Geography. You'd hand her a penny to look at her. In jeans and a jumper Sunday and Monday. Thanks be to God Joan wasn't alive to see her. Useless trying to sleep again.

• • •

Kate thought Mrs Moloney would have to go. Ridiculous to be paying her when she herself was out night cleaning. In the four years since her mother's death how things had changed! The bus bumped along the potholed road ... No traffic jam at this hour of the morning but give it another half hour and the scramble would be on for the rest of the day. How embarrassing to run into Sylvia Doyle in Bewley's last night. Sylvia in her designer outfit and extravagant jewellery.

'As bohemian as ever, I see,' she'd remarked as her eyes slid over Kate's worn jeans and drab jumper.

Sylvia entertained her with tales of her businessman husband and the wonders of the Montessori method of education. Her four children were at a Montessori school. Kate said she was researching a book. A lie, to prevent further probing.

'You were always so clever Kate, but is there money in Geography books?'

'Not much.'

The meeting with Sylvia had diminished her in some way she couldn't fathom.

• • •

'Answer me,' Kate's voice was loud and angry.

Frank moved his gaze from *The Irish Times* to Kate. He stared blankly for a second.

'Scrambled or boiled?' she repeated.

'Scrambled,' and he went back to his newspaper. Kate moved to the cooker.

'Tea's made,' Mrs Moloney said in aggrieved tones.

'Dermot is coming today Dad,' Kate said as she put the scrambled eggs in front of him. No reaction. She was used to being ignored by him. She was looking forward to her brother Dermot's visit. At least it would give her the chance to share her worries about Frank.

Surely Dermot would agree to pay for him to dry out. She looked at her father. He was attempting and failing to fork some scrambled egg to his mouth. His hand shook and the egg fell onto his plate. She heard herself say,

'Daddy.'

She hadn't called him Daddy since schooldays. He looked at her, then at his plate and left the table, stiffly formal.

In his room, he climbed into the bed fully dressed, the hood of the bedclothes obliterating the daylight. He sobbed his shame into his fists, his teeth grazing his knuckles.

'Daddy.'

She must have followed him. Her voice was low and patient.

'I'm not feeling the best this morning Kate. I think I'll sleep for a while. I think I'm in for a bout of 'flu.'

His voice reached her muffled by the bedclothes. She moved to the bed, sat on it, rubbed his hip through the blankets.

'Daddy, you haven't been well for a long time. You know you haven't. I've tried to talk to you before but you wouldn't listen. When Dermot comes today we'll have to talk about getting you medical help. I can't manage on my own anymore.'

She waited for a movement, a word. None came.

• • •

In the kitchen she emptied the cold scrambled eggs into the dustbin. She couldn't eat when Frank didn't. How many meals had she skipped recently? Too many.

'Wasting good food.'

Mrs Moloney made her jump.

'Is your father not feeling well?'

The voice, maliciously bright, gave Kate a tight feeling in her chest.

'You know very well, Mrs Moloney, that Frank hasn't been well for ages. You also know what's wrong with him.'

• • •

Kate climbed to her attic room. Rugs scattered the wooden floor in bold colours. The single bed stood in the middle of the floor, a patchwork quilt of Mexican design covered it, reaching the floor on either side. Three windows lit the room which faced onto the back garden. She took off her shoes and got under the quilt. She felt too anxious to sleep. Everything was sliding out of her control. She was tired of trying to manage on her own. Dermot would have to take some of the responsibility from now on.

If only Jim Lambourne would answer her letters. He put down the phone on her as soon as he heard her voice. It was Frank's fault that he'd gone. Herself and Jim worked in the garden all last year and up to a few days ago.

Frank said once too often, 'What's he hanging around here for? You'd think he'd be glad to get out of the place when his day's work is done.' Jim was shy. At first he said he didn't want to take her out but soon she got round him. Love made everything better until Frank lost the run of himself during Hallowe'en when she hid his last bottle of whiskey. He turned on Jim.

'Do you think you're special? You're a gardener, that's all. When the gardens are in order her ladyship will dismiss you. She's only waiting for the glasshouse plants to be forced for Christmas.'

Jim would not listen to her protests. He simply left and didn't come back. She hadn't slept or eaten properly since then and it was now the third week in December. The day after he'd left, she found the plants in the glasshouse in shambles. She tried to rescue some of them. The hyacinths he'd been forcing for Christmas, their blues and purples were bleeding like open wounds. She did not mind too much that the winter roses and the Christmas cacti were destroyed but she cried when she could not rescue the hyacinths. She hadn't menstruated for two months but then she was irregular. It was only since she'd met Jim Lambourne that the idea of a baby had taken hold of her. It occurred to her now, as she lay restless on her bed, that what had upset her about her meeting with Sylvia was not her perfect clothes, the bourgeois lifestyle. It was Sylvia's children she resented.

• • •

She woke to the sound of the telephone ringing. Resisting wakefulness, she covered her ears. It rang on. She finally got out of bed to answer it.

'Hello Kate, this is Dermot. I won't be able to make it today. I have to be in Brussels by six this evening. A meeting I can't get out of, I'm afraid. But Maria and myself will definitely make it next week for Christmas.'

'Are you sure you can't come?' as if Dermot ever changed his mind when it suited him. The line went silent for a few seconds.

'It's out of my control.'

'Dad is out of control.'

He ignored this. 'I'll see you next week, then, as arranged. Got to rush. I'm chairing a meeting in ten minutes.'

She stood holding the phone even after he'd hung up. She stared at the mouthpiece. Only then did she become aware of the wet feeling between her legs. The blood flecked her white panties.

• • •

Frank could feel them walking up his neck, making for his throat. An army of them. They seemed sure and confident. The mousetraps had failed, so had the poison. He closed his eyes firmly, tightened the bedclothes about him and began laughing quietly, cradling his arms like a child.

The Virgin

by Trudy Hayes

I suppose my life isn't really miserable. Here I am lying in bed smoking a joint. My shirt and trousers lie on the floor beside me. My room is small, untidy, sufficient for my humble needs. Down the road is my studio. I am content, have no great ambitions. No doubt I smoke too much dope.

I get up and put the kettle on for a cup of tea and light a cigarette. I smoke too much but I thoroughly enjoy each cigarette. Above my head hangs a crucifix – a grim and cheerless image but the dreadful love that inspired the death of Christ makes me feel guilty, terribly ashamed of my sins and weaknesses. But oh I wish I could find love! I think sex is sinful, yet cannot do without it. We're all programmed to create our likeness, but I take good care not to do so. Condoms – I don't want to catch AIDS either.

I suppose I'd better get something to eat before I go out. I think I'll go and see Lisa today. I put on a few sausages and when they are cooked I make a hot dog and eat my meal. Before I go I examine myself in the mirror...

I'm tall and slim and I wear my hair in a ponytail. I'm pleasing to women. My face is soft and gentle – no way assertive, but a lot of women like me. Most men are conditioned to be predators – competitive and aggressive and no doubt a lot of women still go for this primitive type. In fact I think I bring out the predator in women.

Outside it is bright and sunny. Lisa lives around the

corner, and I stroll leisurely towards her flat. And yet what beasts men are. I cannot help looking at women as they pass by – gazing at their thighs, their bare arms. I fantasise about women – I cannot help it. I'm sure most men do. Women are so soft, so vulnerable, so delicious.

Finally I arrive. The windows of the flat are open so I know that Lisa is in. I press the button and she answers the door dressed in a tie-dye shirt and baggy trousers.

'Hi' she says, smiling and I know she is stoned. I go inside and we sit on her bed. She lights some incense and puts on a tape. She lies down on the bed beside me and I put my arms around her. Lisa is, I suppose, a hippy. She does nothing, but lives on the dole and smokes dope and eats lentils. She is shy – not good with people and not very intelligent, but occasionally she makes a perceptive remark. She likes sex. I knew that immediately I saw her dancing. She brought me home and we made love in her large double bed. She's a bit fat really – she should take some exercise. She has lots of lovers and needs sex constantly which she believes is good for her.

'How are you?' she asks sleepily.

'Fine' I reply, stroking her arms. I kiss her and she begins to take off her clothes. I disrobe and we make love on the bed and then we lie still. But afterwards I must take a shower, and I do so feeling faintly disgusted as I always do after making love – faintly repelled by a woman's passion. Women, who should be somehow pure and sexless are always shocking in their ardour and my own sexuality disgusts me too. I wrap a towel around me and walk back into Lisa's room.

'Tea?' she asks, opening her sleepy eyes.

'Mmmmmmm,' I reply and she gets up, naked, and walks into the kitchen. This room is so indolent and peaceful. A hippie's haven. Here I could dissolve into non-being, cease to think, to ponder on the universe. Outside of here questions vex me, torment my mind. I wonder why God gave us the treacherous gift of reason which can only lead us to question his omnipotence but I try to suppress my reason and trust in faith – trust in the all-embracing love of God. But in this room there is no reason to strain for truth and logic. I sink down into the bed and watch as Lisa comes back into the room with two cups of tea. She settles down beside me and we smoke cigarettes. I relax into this warm, vacant cocoon and we sit in companionable silence for we rarely speak. My relationship with Lisa is largely physical.

Lisa has tanned, velvety skin. She lies asleep beside me and her breath gently caresses my hand. I stretch lazily on the bed. I wonder what Lisa does all day. I suppose she just smokes dope and watches the television. Curious to have no ambition – it is either very strong or very weak people who have no ambition. People who do not feel they have to prove themselves or people who do not have the confidence to prove themselves. Ambition is fuelled either by insecurity or egotism – or, perhaps, the desire for love. Lisa loves herself, is content with herself – or perhaps she is lazy. Yet the reason I come to her is because of the peace that surrounds her and of course she is beautiful – voluptuous, but in bed she is not beautiful, but wild. It is not right somehow – a woman should not be so passionate.

Lisa has a Crucifix on the wall but she does not really believe. She sits up – naked and shameless.

'Would you like some dope?' she asks.

'Sure' I reply.

She rolls a joint – sticks the skins together and carefully rolls the tobacco between her fingers, then burns some hash. Soon the joint is lighting and she is pulling on it, satisfied. I take a drag and sink even deeper into the bed. I'm being very lazy today. I should be at my easel. I am painting a picture of the Virgin Mary, trying to capture her goodness, her purity, her sinlessness. She is dressed in white – virginal white, and I have tried to paint her eyes full of love.

But the real reason I paint is to celebrate God, to give glory to God. I have painted the Crucifixion many times, but now I am painting the Virgin Mary in all her celestial purity. I am trying to capture her radiance and goodness and have painted her in a long, white robe, her tiny feet like doves beneath her dress, her arms stretched out. And yet I'm such a hypocrite! Here I am sitting in a woman's room after having sinned with her. Here's Lisa now.

'What are you doing for the day?' asks Lisa, sitting down beside me. 'I'm going to cook some lunch. Will you stay?'

'Sure,' I reply.

Cooking – women's work. But I am hungry. Lisa is a wonderful cook and I can look forward to a feast.

Lisa gets up and puts on her dress and combs her long hair. She looks peaceful and innocent, and she turns around and smiles at me. The smile tears at my heart. It is the trusting smile of a child. And yet I cannot love her. I cannot love a woman who indulges in such carnal lust, who abandons herself so completely to passion. Lisa continues brushing her hair, gazing dreamily at her reflection in the mirror.

'What are you thinking about?' she asks, swinging around.

'Nothing,' I reply. 'Just that you're beautiful.'

Lisa stands up and walks over towards me and I kiss her.

'Love me?' she asks.

'Yes,' I reply, looking into her eyes. She is stoned. She wraps her arms around me, but I push her away. I cannot face any more love-making.

'Put on a tape,' I say, and she does so.

'OK,' she says. 'But I'll cook some lentils now.'

She walks out of the bedroom and I relax back on the bed and examine the bookshelf. Not a great reader. Lisa doesn't have an analytical mind and she doesn't worry about the meaning of the universe. Conversation with Lisa is relaxed, easy-going – she does not have strong opinions and her passivity is sometimes irritating. But I am sure God loves her. Yet I am sure it is sinful to sleep with her and deep within me I am angry with her – angry because she has me within her power, because she arouses my desire. I lead quite a blameless life except that I sin against God by sleeping with women who are too beautiful to resist.

'Paul,' says Lisa suddenly from the kitchen. 'Lunch up'.

I walk into the kitchen and sit down. Lisa dishes up a kind of stew made of lentils and leeks and bean-sprouts – quite delicious. She sits opposite me, eating and looking dreamily into space. The kitchen is full of plants, and leads out into the back garden which is wild and overgrown.

'Any plans for the day?' I ask.

'Not really,' replies Lisa.

'Why don't we go for a drink?' I ask.

'Sure,' replies Lisa.

There is no further conversation. She's really not very intelligent, not very bright. After we have finished eating Lisa makes a pot of tea and we sit in silence smoking cigarettes. Lisa looks satisfied and utterly relaxed. She makes no demands, seems content in my company, makes little conversation.

Afterwards I stand up to wash the dishes in the cramped little sink. I pour some washing-up liquid on the few plates and knives and forks, but then decide to leave the washing-up for Lisa. I stare out the window. Lisa is quite happy to pass through life without her name in the history books. She does not crave fame, fortune, success, excitement, but is sufficient unto herself and I admire her self-possession. I walk back into the bedroom.

'Are we right?' I ask.

'OK,' says Lisa. 'I'll just throw some clothes on.'

She puts on an old blue dress which has seen better days and a pair of sandals, then ties her hair back. Outside it is a lovely evening – a calm summer evening. We go to the Harbour Bar in Bray and sit contentedly sipping pints.

'It's a beautiful night,' remarks Lisa, who has an irritating habit of making inane remarks.

'Yes,' I agree. 'You look lovely.'

Even in an old blue dress with her hair tied back Lisa looks lovely. She is all gentleness, all softness, yet so wild, so passionate in bed. I am looking forward to making love to her tonight – and yet I dread it – I dread damnation.

'Will we go for a walk along the beach?' asks Lisa.

'Sure,' I agree.

We finish off our pints and walk along by the beach.

I take Lisa in my arms and kiss her and her mouth is warm and soft. I pull her towards me, her body soft and maddeningly beautiful. Relentlessly I kiss her and she moans ever more passionately. But a woman should not abandon herself utterly to sensuality. I kiss her sandy, golden skin and caress her with frantic hands. To think that I am risking my very soul for a woman. I put my hands on her breasts and when I caress her she moans with pleasure – a corrupt, fallen woman lying on the sand in my arms.

2

Today I feel somehow serene. I have kept away from women all week and have been working on my portrait of the Virgin Mary. And yet the image does not reflect the splendour of the image in my head. I wish I was more gifted so that I could do the Virgin justice. Imagine the joy in the Virgin's breast when she heard from the angel Gabriel that she was to give birth to the son of God!

I am going to call on June today. I arrive at her flat and knock – Number 4 Brooke Road. She answers wearing a short green dress. She always manages to look virginal even though she tries to look sexy.

'Hello my long-haired lover,' she says, quite glad to see me. 'Come inside and delight me with your wit and scintillating conversation. I haven't seen anyone for weeks.'

'And how's the artist?' I enquire.

'Great,' she replies. I follow her into the living room. There are books everywhere. June wants to be a writer. She is intelligent, and I think, very talented. I don't know what she sees in me. But it is my gift – pleasing women. I sit down and June sits down opposite me, perched on her seat.

'How's the painting going?' she asks.

'Fine,' I reply.

'What are you painting?' she asks.

'The Virgin Mary,' I reply.

'You must be crazy,' she says. 'Who wants to look at religious images? The cult of the Virgin Mary, is in any case, oppressive to women.'

We argue about religion, and the conversation becomes quite heated. June is exciting to talk to – full of challenging ideas and original insights but she is a little too opinionated. And yet despite her cleverness and talent June lacks confidence in herself. I think she thinks she has something to prove to the world. She is slightly insecure, slightly paranoid. And she is, like Lisa, irresistible.

'Obviously your masculinity is threatened by sexually assertive women,' says June.

I pull her towards me, grinning.

'Submit to me, woman, or I'll tie you to the kitchen sink,' I say.

Laughing, she comes to me and sits on my knee.

We sit and chat and she gets up to put on a record.

'Hey! Kitchen slave!' I say. 'Come and give me a kiss.'

June walks over to me and puts her arms around me. She seems genuinely glad to see me – genuinely happy to be in my arms. I hug her to me – she is somehow more vulnerable than Lisa, despite her cleverness. She should learn how to relax – be less assertive.

We make love and afterwards I hate her – loathe her. I hate her femininity, her beauty, the uninhibited pleasure she takes in sin.

'Give me a cigarette,' says June, leaning up on one arm.

I pass her a cigarette and she nonchalantly lights it and blows a stream of smoke at the ceiling. I pick up a cigarette and light it too but I feel terrible.

'Cheer up,' says June. June sits and her hair tumbles over her shoulders. She taps her cigarette, reaching out a slender arm.

'Hi gorgeous,' she says and I try to smile but I cannot let go of the self-loathing. How I despise myself – how weak I am to have sinned again – what kind of man am I that I cannot contain my lechery? And what kind of woman is June that she gives in to such debauchery? She should be chaste and a virgin. But we live in an increasingly Godless world. How terrible that God sacrificed his only son to save sinners and no-one thinks about Christ any more. People do not think about death either. The momentum of life takes over, I suppose, and we forget that we are mortal ...

3

I think I'll go and visit Kay today who I haven't seen for ages. I met Kay in a pub with some friends and she spent the evening talking to me and then she invited me home – she's a bit tarty really. Within seconds she had made her intentions clear and I ended up in bed with her. Kay works for a publishing house and leads a glamorous life going to launches and meeting famous writers. She is strikingly beautiful, determined and ambitious and most men are frightened of her because they feel castrated by her.

I walk out to Serpent Avenue and knock on Number 69. Kay answers the door dressed in a black dress patterned with white butterflies. She has just washed her hair, which falls to her shoulders in waves.

'Come in my handsome prince,' she says, and I step

inside, my feet sinking into the soft, luxurious carpet. I walk into the living-room and sit into a leather armchair while Kay puts on some music.

'Drink?' she asks, floating past me.

'Whiskey,' I reply. She pours out two drinks and then sits down and smiles. She looks like a Vogue model – unavailable, and yet I have held her in my arms while she cried out in passion.

The flat is lit by discreet lamps, and I feel like an intruder in this designer apartment.

'How are you?' asks Kay.

'Wonderful,' I reply. 'Have you been pining for me?'

'Not at all,' she replies, smiling. 'I've been frantically busy. Shall we go for a meal? I'm hungry.'

'Sure,' I reply. 'Let's go for a Chinese.'

'OK,' replies Kay. She puts on a long black coat, and, looking extremely dramatic, she walks out ahead of me. I feel like a distinctly inappropriate companion in my jeans and jumper. Kay stops a taxi and we drive through the city to 'The Lobster Pot'. Soon we are seated and eating delicious Chinese food – it is one of the most expensive restaurants in Dublin.

'So how's my expert lover?' inquires Kay, smiling.

'Well,' I reply.

'I hope you are going to stay the night,' says Kay.

'Sure,' I reply. Kay is delightfully straightforward. Soon her eyes are sparkling and her cheeks are flushed with wine. The black and white dress falls off her shoulders and I am astonished at her beauty, astonished that I can possess this woman, that she wants me to make love to her. She leans forward to talk to me. Her shoulders are round and soft and her voice is gently mocking.

She tells me about her adventures in the publishing

world – about uncooperative authors and incompetent editors. The evening passes quickly and then I take Kay by the arm (she is slightly drunk) and I bring her home in a taxi. We arrive at her flat and she giggles as she searches for her key and fumbles with it before opening the door and kissing me in the hallway.

'You're my favourite,' she says, swaying against me and leading me into the living room. She puts on some music and begins to dance, her body flowing to the music. Kay always gets ecstatically happy when she's drunk. She throws her arms open to me and I walk over to her.

'Kiss me,' she says and I bend my head and kiss her deeply. I pull her dress down off her shoulders and unzip it at the back.

'Come,' says Kay and I follow her into the bedroom. The room is painted black and beside the bed is an orange lamp shade. She pulls me towards her and I cannot resist ...

In the morning I wake up and get up quickly. I cannot face talking to the woman I have sinned with and I feel unhappy and bewildered. I go downstairs and open the fridge, then take out a carton of orange juice and pour out a glass, which refreshes me. The fridge is well stocked and I could stay and prepare a magnificent breakfast but somehow I cannot rest easy with myself – I feel too tormented by guilt. Kay's cat stares bleakly at me, no doubt looking for a glass of milk. She rubs against my legs and I stoop to kiss her, then pour out a saucer of milk. The kitchen gleams – it is magnificently clean and modern.

I leave a note for Kay and then leave the flat, closing the door softly behind me. Disconsolately I walk into town, into Bewley's and get myself a cup of coffee. I feel I have reached some sort of crisis in my life.

Finally I have decided to make a choice between good and evil – between women and God. My painting is nearly finished and I am putting the final touches to it as the sun streams in the window.

The Virgin Mary shimmers before me and I feel ecstatic. Her eyes are full of love for suffering humanity, and a glittering tear flows on her cheek. But through her tears she smiles. Her gown cascades in folds of azure blue to her feet, which are like doves. Finally I have finished – nearly finished the painting. I contemplate it with bliss in my heart – I have painted the essence of purity.

The other paintings I have painted lie scattered around the room and they seem dull and pointless in comparison with my painting of the Virgin Mary. I can almost feel her presence in the room, the presence of goodness. I put the finishing touches to the painting and then stand back. The Virgin smiles at me and I watch in horror as she steps down from the canvas and walks up to me.

'It wasn't true,' she says gently.

'It wasn't an immaculate conception.'

Divided Attention

by Mary Morrissy

He rang first three months ago – at three in the morning. The phone blundered into my fogged brain and I lay in bed not sure if the burring was in my ears or the vestige of a dream phone. But then, phones in dreams ring, don't they? They're usually old, black Bakelite models – as if the fixtures of our dreams are awaiting modernisation. It continued for several minutes, not a demon of sleep but a whimpering child waiting to be picked up. Alarmed and sour with sleep, I padded to the kitchen. It could only be death at this hour, death or bad news, or ... you. I shook the thought away. I was no longer a woman waiting for the phone to ring. I lifted the receiver.

'Hello?'

Silence.

'Hello?' I heard my own puzzled tone echo back at me.

Still nothing.

'Hello?' Mild aggravation now – I know that tone from the receiving end.

'Who is this?'

The silence persisted. Why is it so disconcerting on the phone? Why does it yawn so? Minutes gape.

'Hello!'

There was a shifting sound. I got the impression of a large bulk wedged into a small space. Then an exerted breathing. It was laboured, distressed even. Was someone hurt, wounded in some way? I conjured up pictures of a street fight, or a mugging, a man stumbling into a phone box clutching a bloody side and dialling the first number that came into his head. Was it someone I knew? Victor, I thought. A friend of mine, an asthmatic with a comic book name, prone to late night, melancholy drinking. You wouldn't know him. When he is distressed he makes this gnawing sound, a device he uses to reassure himself that he will draw the next lungful.

'Victor, is that you, Victor?'

The breathing intensified, louder now, more protesting.

'Are you all right, Victor? Are you hurt? What's wrong?'

There was a harrumphing noise like a horse snorting and the breathing shifted up a gear, quicker, more jagged. I heard in it a rising panic, an urgency that had not been there before. And then, only then, I realised. This was an obscene phone call. I slammed the receiver down. I was shaking. The phone sat there, implacable. Flat as a pancake, the little square buttons in their serried rows, the receiver safely in its snug depressions, the letter-box window stoutly declaring my number, the coy curl of its flex. How often had I sat staring at it, willing it to ring, cursing it for its refusal. But then it had been a co-conspirator, imbued with a delicious imminence as if it too was longing to hear from you. It was traitorous sometimes, but never *this*, never spiteful. Now it had invited a pervert into my home. How could I ever trust it again?

You would have said, change your number, that's what you would have said. I know exactly the tone you would use – emphatic, overlaid with a professional concern. You managed that combination well. A sort of alms-giving affection. Go ex-directory, you would have said, like me. What a relief, you once said, no more crank calls. Precisely! You didn't know I had your number, did you? I got it by stealth. Oh, I looked in the directory hoping to find your name there carelessly among impostors. There are five who share your name in the book, all of whom could have been you but none of whom were. I pitied those who were not you; I pitied anyone who thought one of these frauds was you. But that was early on. It was only later that I pitied myself.

It started innocently, I swear. I had not intended ever to use your number. Having it alone was enough. I carried it around in my wallet, taking it out from time to time and contemplating it, wondering what it would be like for this particular conjunction of figures to be familiar – oh, let's not beat around the bush – to be *mine*. I wanted them to spell out home. It soothed me to have it; it was connection, that was all, just connection. And it served as my lucky charm, like a rabbit's foot, which had the power to conjure you up and granted me an ownership which you knew nothing about. As long as I had your number, *I* would be safe.

Celia told me to report the call.

'You must protect yourself,' she said. Her stout face flushed angrily, her perm bounced. 'The bastard.'

Much like what she said of you.

You once remarked that she had the sort of looks that would have won a bonny baby competition, ruddy cheeks, plump arms, a stolid, ready smile, those curls. Can't you see her in bonnet and pantaloons, you said. Watch the birdie, Celia! I used to smile when I saw her and remembered that, a sly, complicitous smile, a smile for *you*. It was part of our language, the secret, mocking language of lovers. Now I look at Celia squarely in the face and think – she is here; you are not.

I didn't report it, I don't know why. Laziness, perhaps, embarrassment. But no, it was more than that. I was resisting this man, and his method of entry into my life. I didn't want him to force me into changing my number. I didn't want him to have the power to make me fear my own telephone. I didn't want the notion of him to make any difference to me – echoes, echoes. And anyway, I couldn't bring myself to describe the call. If I put it into words, it would sound flat and neutral. What was it only a series of silences punctuated by heaving and gasping? Who would understand the great gap between what it was and how it made me feel? Perhaps it *had* been Victor? He would ring soon and say shamefacedly 'Look, about the other night ... .'

But the biggest fear was that the policeman logging this call down in the large ledger of misdemeanours would look up at me and know that I too have been a caller in my time.

I rang your number first time as an experiment, simply to see if I could. And I was curious too, about your other life. The Wife, the Two Daughters, the Baby. *She* answered.

'8809682, hello?'

I heard the sun in her voice; it spoke to me of gaiety

and ease. I saw a blond woman, hair scraped back in a workaday ponytail (that you might later loosen), a floral dress, bare legs and sandals. She was slightly out of breath as if she had run in from the garden. In the background a child was wailing. She said 'excuse me' and put her hand over the mouthpiece.

'Emily,' I heard her say, 'give Rachel the teddy. You must learn to share.'

'Hello?' she said again slightly crossly.

I put the phone down swiftly.

Of course, it didn't stop there. Curiosity knows no boundaries. The first call had rewarded me with your daughters' names – you had always referred to them as The children, an anonymous troop of foot soldiers. But then, I suppose, my name was never uttered in your household.

I picked times when I knew you wouldn't be there. You see, it was not you I wanted, but your world. Sometimes, Emily – or was it Rachel?- answered. They would deliver your number in a piping voice before the receiver was taken away. I got to know the sounds of your house. Your doorbell has chimes. Your hallway has no carpet – I have heard the tinny crash of toys falling on a hard surface. The television is in a room close to the phone. I have heard its muffled explosions, the clatter and boom of cartoons before your wife says: 'Emily, *please* shut the door.'

He rang again. Same time. He's a creature of habit. This time I was awake. I had come in from a party – yes, I'm getting out now, mixing, meeting people. I was making coffee. There was a vague drumming in my temples that would later become a hangover. I was still in my finery, or some of it. I had kicked off my shoes and was removing my earrings when the phone trilled. I lifted it and knew immediately it was him. The quality of *his* silence is different; it is the silence of ambush. This time I said nothing, remembering with shame my response the first time, my babbling concern for Victor which had exposed me as a stupid woman who didn't recognise an obscene call even in the middle of it. I thought too that if I said nothing, *he* would be forced to speak.

As time went by, I got more adventurous, or desperate. I rang once at three a.m. – the witching hour! Nothing malicious, I promise; I simply wanted to hear your voice. You answered almost immediately. There must be another phone by the bed. You must have been awake. Perhaps you had just made love to her and you were having a cigarette, resting the ashtray on your chest and blowing smoke rings into the air, your arm lazily around her shoulder. *This* I know.

'Hello?' you said.

'Larry,' I heard her whisper, 'who is it?'

Larry, she calls you Larry.

And then, there was another sound. The gurgling of a baby, the drowsy, drugged stirrings of a child suckling. The night feed.

'Don't know,' I heard you say thoughtfully.

Was that suspicion in your voice?

I imagined you withdrawing your arm from around her.

'Just a wrong number,' I heard you say before the line went dead.

They say that with flashers you should laugh at them. Cuts them down to size, literally. But with a caller, my caller, it was more difficult. He operated on my imagination. I wondered what he did in the phone box. (I always thought of him in a phone box though he could have been ringing from the comfort of his own home.) I imagined him fumbling with his fly as I answered, then rubbing himself, abandoning himself to his own grim joy while I listened. He wanted me – anyone – to listen. And what did he get out of it? Horror, fear, abuse maybe. Perhaps that's what drove him on. That was another thing; he never reached a climax. Maybe he couldn't and that was his problem. Or maybe my silence, my intent listening inhibited him.

I remember once hearing my mother make love. She had been out and came home late. I heard the scrape of the key in the lock and the sound of coarse whispering in the hall. The stairs creaked. The loose floorboard in the landing, which I knew how to avoid, groaned. My mother giggled. I imagined her leading someone by the hand, a blind man not familiar with the obstacles of our house – the low chest on the landing, the laundry basket that held the bathroom door ajar. He stumbled against something.

'Shh,' she urged, 'the children!'

I lay, stiff with wakefulness, as they went into her room. A thin wall separated us. In the darkness I manufactured pictures. A skirmish in a cobble square, her bed a high-sprung carriage rocked by a baying crowd. A cry! My mother's sharp and high. Has someone hurled a stone? The crowd sets to with more vigour, heaving, pushing. She cries again but it is muffled as if she is being thrown against the coach's soft upholstery. I hear the tramp of boots on oily cobbles – left, right, left, right – the icy whip of bayonets, the vicious sheen of blades. A groan. He staggers; she cries out 'no!' I hammer with my fists against the wall. Stop, stop!

I rang the night of the party. New Year. Tradition, you said, we always have a crowd in. You looked at me ruefully.

'I'd much prefer to be with you, you know that.' You shrugged.

I called close to midnight. A guest answered. I felt safe to speak your name.

'Hold on,' she said gaily, 'I'll get Laurence. Laurence ... it's for you.' The receiver was put down. For several minutes I was a gatecrasher at your party. Oh, how festive it sounded! There was a noisy crescendo of conversation, the ring of laughter, a male voice above the din calling plaintively, 'the opener, has anyone seen the bottle opener?'

I saw plates of steaming food being handed across a crowded room, glasses foaming at the rim, streamers trailing from your hair.

'Hello!' you cried triumphantly – several drinks on. 'Excuse the noise. Party!'

I could have spoken then but I didn't. What would I have said? Happy New Year from a well-wisher. No, then you would have known the power I had over you, the power to betray *you*.

'Oops,' I heard a woman cry, 'Careful!'

I didn't, of course, betray you. But knowing that I could

changed things. I had to stop ringing for fear I would blurt it out – our secret. The snatched moments, the meetings in pubs, the subterfuge. Instead, I have to admit it, I went to your house. Just once. Once was enough.

It was night, I took the train. I crossed the metal bridge at your station imagining your gaze on its familiar struts. The stationmaster snoozed in his booth, his chin resting on his soiled uniform. He didn't check my ticket. This made me feel invisible, convinced me that I wasn't really doing this – making a pilgrimage to the shrine of your home. You see, even at the height of what I felt for you I realised how foolish I'd become, how it reduced me. A rush of embarrassment overcame me. I almost heard the singing of the rails as another train approached, the train on which the fading spectre of my sensible alter ego should have travelled back to the city. I turned my back on her.

I picked my way through the quiet, darkening streets, their paths shaded by the crowning canopies of ancient trees, whose burgeoning roots tore the paving stones asunder. It was late spring, fragrant after rain. Petals floated in the kerbside puddles. A fresh breeze soughed in the trees. I passed the lighted windows of other homes. Their warm, rosy rooms were on display – the haloes of standard lamps, tangles of greenery, the flickering, livid-blue glow of unwatched televisions. Sometimes I glimpsed a family tableau. A father in an armchair, one child on his lap, another perched on the armrest. A granny with a walking-frame and sagging face – a stroke victim, I guessed – being hauled to her feet by a young woman plump with goodness. Two blonde girls sitting cross-legged on a window seat plaiting one another's hair.

You live on a high, sloping avenue overlooking the bay. The lights of the city jostled on the skyline, beacons flooding the water with silent messages, mouthing like goldfish. I approached your house like a thief, slipping into the garden with darting looks up and down the street. I cringed at the creak of the gate, slipping quickly around it to hide behind the large oak, the only tree in the garden. I leaned gratefully against its bark. There was a muddled bare patch at its base as if it had sheltered others before me and I knew I would find hearts and arrows carved on its trunk. Your house stands on its own. Pleasing, symmetrical, five windows around an arched doorway. It was ablaze with light. I must have stood there for hours growing chilled and stiff as the night closed in, the sky turning to indigo. The swift stealth of the moon threw the garden into relief.

I was rewarded – finally. The front door opened. An orange beam of light flooded down the path. I peered from my fronds of shadow. And then your voice.

' ... and then it's straight to bed!'

You were holding the hand of a dark-haired child of about five. Rachel, or at least I decided it was Rachel.

'Amn't I a good girl, Daddy, amn't I?!'

'Yes, of course you are.'

'Am I your favourite?'

A dog bounded down the garden. I froze. You never told me you had a dog. He frisked on the lawn and Rachel whooped delightedly.

'Look, Daddy, look at Brandy!' (Brandy – what a name for a dog. Why didn't you go the whole hog and call it Smirnoff?) Brandy trailed towards the gate.

'Brandy, Brandy,' you called.

I stiffened, fearing the dog would smell the stranger in your midst and would expose me, panting victoriously at my feet. I imagined you finding me there, cowering in the undergrowth. How could I explain? There was no explanation except that I wanted to see you. I held my breath, terrified. You were close now. I could smell *you*, but it seemed that I had stood there for so long that my odour of fear and longing had been taken up by the very veins of the leaves and belonged now to the garden itself. Rachel saved me.

'Daddy,' she wailed. 'Daddy, where are you? I can't see you.'

'It's all right, darling, I'm here.'

'Daddy?"

'It's okay.' You halted, a hair's breadth away. 'I'm still here.'

You turned away and walked into a sudden shaft of moonlight. Seeing you thus, I ached to be discovered, to share in the tenderness you saved for this little girl. The dog scampered up the path ahead of you. Rachel rushed out of the gloom and clung to your waist. You lifted her up and carried her inside drawing the train of light in after you. The door closed.

I was alone, shut out where I belonged, in the pit of the garden.

I've told all this to the caller. I've named him Larry in your honour. I've had to battle against his groaning and heaving but I've persisted. He keeps ringing so it must do something for him. It's therapy for me, you could say. Therapy, indeed! I can see you wrinkle your nose distainfully. I needed to tell someone. I needed to tell *you* – but he's a good second best. I address the noisy static that is his frustration. I am happier that he is preoccupied – as you were in your way – and that he is not listening exclusively to me. I could not bear undivided attention.

Last week I threw your number away. The paper on which it was written was yellowed and grubby and ragged along the folds. The ink had almost faded away. I found it had lost its power. Does this mean I'm cured? Of you, perhaps.

Seduced

by Ivy Bannister

'Oh, Vincent O'Toole,' she says, 'It's magic the way the stars twinkle down upon us.'

You can see the stars, here and there, through the crumbling roof of the derelict warehouse he calls home and studio. They lie, Calley and Vincent, companionable strangers on his straw mattress, where the fluttering of her body has made him drowsy.

'Oh, Vincent O'Toole,' she says, 'I love you so much,' and she locks her slender leg over his substantial thigh.

'So much?' he teases. He doesn't believe Calley since he scarcely knows her. Instead, he seizes a fistful of her dark curls, admiring the way they bounce back into shape when he lets go. Resilient, he thinks. It's a word that he likes.

'Beliefs are important,' she says. 'I believe that every star in the sky has the soul of a baby.' Her eyes glow like mother-of-pearl in the dark, but he's too sleepy to notice. 'So many stars,' she whispers, ' so many babies.'

'Why don't we talk in the morning?' Vincent O'Toole turns over and falls asleep. Together, they float in a sea of shadows and space, watched over by the hulking outlines of Vincent's many possessions.

When the morning light has flooded the warehouse, Vincent reaches for the woman, but next to him the mattress has gone cold. Without getting up, he peers among the canvases and buckets and plastic sheeting, between the tyres and silvery sand, the sieves and barrows and bins, the trunks and rusty trolleys, throughout the jungle of homeless objects that he collects for his art. Improbably, Calley spots him first, alert to his darting eye. 'Vincent,' she calls. Her voice pipes like a birdsong among the bright treasures. There she is, enthroned upon an armchair, a striking figure in her red Indian dress, splashed over the green brocade, a heady display of colour and texture. Her black curls tumble about her gaunt face and shoulders. As he looks, he sees a Florentine madonna, transported from the fourteenth century. But wait. Something is askew in the image. Her skinny elbows bob like a chicken flapping its wings.

'What the hell are you doing?' he enquires.

'Knitting.'

'What the hell for?'

'Our baby.'

Vincent laughs, his morning crankiness quite dispelled by this whimsy. The idea of himself as father is ludicrous.

He bounces up, bull-keen to tackle the day, and washes with rainwater from a bucket. As he slaps the cold water onto his chest, he stands astride, his huge thighs glistening, a colossus in his warehouse; and he tells Calley his story about the farmer and the three-legged chicken. It's a good laugh, but she isn't amused.

He is not put out. The girls he brings home are all sorts, and he doesn't give a damn for their sense of humour. It was last night he picked Calley up. He'd nearly squashed her, a frail insect, as she'd hovered on the footpath outside his local. He'd thought she was a child, but when she turned her plaintive face full upon him, he'd seen a waif-woman with an enigmatic smile, so he'd invited her back to share his roof for the night. Why shouldn't he? Was he not Vincent O'Toole,

Saviour, Superman and Healer of Strays?

'Well, Calley,' he says now, in his best cowboy drawl, 'I'm gonna rustle you up some breakfast.' She inclines her head towards him, but she keeps on knitting.

This knitting irritates him. Who ever saw a madonna knit? 'If you have to knit,' he suggests, 'knit something useful. Socks for instance.' He imagines a mountain of socks, a huge fluffy mound of startling colours. 'Yes,' he tells her, 'make me some socks. Something bizarre. Something amusing. Why not orange socks?'

'When I finish this baby jacket,' she answers, flapping her elbows.

'Baby jacket,' he mutters. 'Pah!' He retreats from its horrible pinkness into his beloved larder. Behind a partition, he has refashioned the country store of his boyhood. He believes in quantities of preserved food, as a declaration of faith in tomorrow. He intends never to run out. His tins are stacked densely upon the shelves. Tin after tin, rows of soldiers, labels spattered with damp, yellowing from age. Stew and corned beef with peas. Beans galore. Pear halves, pineapple pieces and smiling mandarin segments. Bottles of beer, lemonade, chutney and tomato sauce. Enormously happy in his larder, Vincent begins to sing.

In the town where I was born ...
Lived a man who sailed the sea...

He taps out the rhythm as he lights his battered bottled gas cooker.

Into the skillet go the sausages. Snip, snip, snip. Plump as a fat lady's fingers, they shiver and jump, mingling juices with the hot oil. The smell makes Vincent salivate. With a flourish, he cracks the eggs.

And he told us of his life ...
In the land of submarines ...

The yellowy egg hearts throb in the whitening albumen, and Vincent's stomach rumbles. Contentedly, he hacks blood purple wedges from a loop of black pudding.

As he cooks, he dreams of painting Calley. Calley in a panorama of monster lorries, meathooks, carcasses and smashed aircraft. Calley, his stray from a Florentine fresco, overwhelmed by technology. Calley, sacrificed on the altar of modern machinery.

Delighted with his idea, Vincent ladles breakfast onto two plates. By now, he is ravenous. His inspiration knits in the green brocade chair. He studies her with pride in his plans for her. 'It's ready,' he cries, exhilarated by his power. He slaps the plates down on the trestle table. But Calley is slow to join him.

'I can't paint without a good breakfast,' he complains. She rises ever so slowly, Calley from the sea, wafting towards him on a scallop shell. She strolls over. He is amazed to see her knit while she walks, her bony little fingers speeding back and forth, in and out. Faster than a croupier counting money with an agile forefinger. Bony but steely.

She is nearly at the table. Vincent sits, seizing his own knife and fork. She stands beside him, so slight of stature, that her face is barely above his.

'I can't eat this junk,' she says.

'Pardon?'

She slops his cup of tea into a rainwater bucket. 'I'm doing you a favour,' she says. 'D'you know what's in it? Tannic acid. That junk would atrophy your insides. And you an artist. You should be ashamed of using stimulants. Did Leonardo da Vinci need stimulants? Of course not. He didn't want his insides to turn into old shoe leather.'

Vincent stares at her mouth. He wonders at the extravagance of words pouring from such ethereal lips. His fried eggs are going cold. 'Sit down and eat your breakfast,' he grumbles. 'We'll talk later.'

Calley stamps her little foot. 'Have you considered the fat content in that lot? If it congeals on the plate, what's it going to do to your arteries? Do you want to poison the baby?'

'What baby?'

'Our baby. Of course, it's still only a cell or two,' she adds reflectively.

'What are you talking about?'

'You know what I'm talking about.'

She wasn't serious. She couldn't be. How could her sparrow-like frame serve something so vigorous as maternity? 'Besides,' as Vincent adds out loud, 'we only did it once.'

'You only need to do it once. Any teenager knows that. Only we're not teenagers. At least, you're not.' She smiles sweetly before continuing. 'I selected you as father because I like your painting. I realise that this isn't a popular view, but no matter what people say against your work, everyone agrees it's ambitious. And I want our daughter to be an artist ... Naturally, I hope we'll do it more than once.'

Vincent is flummoxed. 'Just tell me one thing. How could you know? How do you know that you're ... well, that it took.'

'I know.' She presses her palms solemnly upon her abdomen.

'Hold on!' Vincent snaps. 'There is no baby! There couldn't be!' The vast space of the warehouse began to wobble about him.

'A love child,' Calley said.

Sweat dribbles down Vincent's neck. 'This is crazy. If I thought you weren't on the pill, I wouldn't have ...'

But Calley interrupts. 'Love children aren't like ordinary children,' she says. 'I read about them in a book. Our little girl will be remarkable.'

The warehouse is now spinning around Vincent, a kaleidoscope of colour and shape. He grabs a cold sausage and bolts it, feeling its nourishment flow down into his stomach.

Calley watches him chew. 'Fat men die younger,' she says.

Flinging his plate to the floor, he rages like a bear. 'I don't like this!' he yells. 'What's more, I don't believe it. You've got to be crazy! ... Besides, you've made me lose my temper. If there's anything I can't stand, it's losing my temper. I'm going out now. When I come back, you'd better be gone.'

As he flees, Calley's voice pursues him. 'You're over-emotional. Even shocked. But everything's going to be ...'

Ignoring her, he flings himself out, squeezing past the barricaded door, tramping through the overgrown yard, for once not caring who might see him. He kicks his way through stink-weed and couch grass. In his path, a brick glints, pink like a snake's eye amid the dandelions. He heaves it back at his squat, watching it float in an arc towards one of the high windows. The glass shatters, with a satisfying crash, and he hears the debris tinkling down among his things.

'Aroint thee, witch!' he bellows, shaking his fist. 'Away! Be gone when I come back!'

He hopes he has frightened her. Outrageous insect!

Had he plucked her out of the gutter to be insulted? To have his breakfast spoiled? To be violated for a madwoman's fantasy? 'Some madonna,' he snarls, determined to shake her out of his head.

The Grand Canal shimmers before him. He begins to walk, snorting the air hard into his lungs, then puffing it out his mouth. His elbows pump, sharp and fast. Power walking, he thinks. His sandals slip and slide. His face turns red. Runners, he thinks. I'm going to have to get myself some runners. In no time at all, he remembers how hungry he is. Tousle-haired and panting, he bursts into a shop so tiny that his prodigious bulk fills it entirely.

Behind the counter, the elderly shopkeeper shies away, rat-eyed with terror. 'Take it! Take every penny!' he squeals, his yellow lips aquiver, his hands tearing the drawer from an ancient register, and dumping its contents out on the counter.

Wild-eyed, Vincent inspects the pile of dog-eared notes and coppers. 'I don't want your money,' he says. 'All I want is bread and a bottle of lemonade.'

The old man shudders. His bulbous nose twitches.

'What's the matter with you?' Vincent asks. 'I don't have two heads. Aren't you going to serve me?'

'You mean you're not one of them hooligans?'

'Pardon?'

'Them mingy little rotters that did me last week.'

'The swine.'

Relieved, the old fella's scrabbling fingers retrieve his miserable funds. Then he pulls up his vest. 'Look at this, Mister,' he says.

The sagging torso is blue-black with bruises, pitted

as if gravel had been ground into it. In his head, Vincent hears the thump of young fists upon old flesh. He shudders. 'It's an evil world we live in,' he mutters. Still, why should the old geezer mistake him, Vincent O'Toole, for a batterer of old men? In some dudgeon, Vincent gathers up his loaf and bottle of lemonade. He is so hungry that he tears off a handful of bread and wads it into his mouth.

'What did they take?' he asks, chewing.

'Everything. If I'd a shotgun, I'd of peppered the buggers.' The old man hawks, his venom-spittle shooting across the counter, but his baldy head droops onto a wheezing chest.

Vincent is fascinated. How awful, he thinks, it must be to grow old. Who could consider it pleasant to share a pillow with such a moth-eaten head? Soberly, Vincent delves into his pocket and pulls out a fiver. 'Here,' he says, 'keep the change.'

A claw-like hand snatches the money. But as Vincent backs out, he sees suspicion, not gratitude, taking root on the old man's face. What's wrong with me today? Vincent worries. Didn't I bring him even a moment's happiness? Have I lost my magical touch?

'Calley,' niggles a voice in the back of his head, but Vincent repudiates it.

Back in the sunshine, Vincent blows the pong of old men out of his nose, and heads for town, wadding bread into his mouth, and scattering crumbs for the birds. He basks in the infinity of greens around him. Green is his favourite colour. He sees it everywhere. Green feathered upon green, emerald upon jade. He would paint the world green, if only he had a brush big enough.

On Baggot Street Bridge, Vincent eagerly inspects the bookshop window. Nothing. He pops in the door with an engaging smile for the proprietor. 'Fine day, Mr O'Toole,' she says. Frisky old bird, he thinks. Buoyant. No chance she'd take him for a hooligan.

'Has it come in yet?' he demands.

'Remind me.'

Vincent says nothing, but plunges back to Poetry, where he spots the slim spine with its gold lettering. What? Only two copies? He seizes them both, and rushes back to the front.

'Look here,' he says. '*Green Out of Chaos*! How's that for a title? Hugh Fennessy.'

'Never heard of him.'

'You will. Listen. This is a man with a future.' The volume falls open in Vincent's hand. He reads expressively, each syllable resonant.

> *'Genghis Khan did slaughter the helpless,*
> *Abandon infants for carrion.*
> *Now the lowly worm has made him fruitful;*
> *Damask roses spring from his loins.*

'Well, what do you think?' he asks.

'Purple,' she chirps. 'Sounds to me like a man with a past.'

Vincent is unperturbed. 'Mark my words. Everyone will be reading this Fennessy man. You'd better re-order. Get up a window display. The public will snap them up.'

'Hah!' she says.

Does he imagine it? Does her spirited eye look at him with particular interest? Has his physical presence tapped a rich memory in her silver-haired head?

'A piece of advice,' he says. 'Keep a copy yourself.

Don't you know what a first edition of early Beckett is worth these days?'

Vincent pays for both copies and strolls out. Across the bridge he sees Bord Fáilte. 'Welcome!' he cries cheerily, 'Welcome indeed!' 'With compliments,' he writes on a flyleaf. 'Hugh Fennessy,' he scrawls, and deposits the book in the letter box. Then Vincent O'Toole, alias Hugh Fennessy, heads jauntily for the city centre.

In the Brobdingnag shadow of Holles Street Hospital, a behemoth-woman waits for the light. No maiden this, but a great tun of female, swollen with pregnancy. Purple veins bulge on piano legs; thick ankles spill over feet in men's shoes. The light gone green, she lumbers across the road, shoving a low-riding pram, bursting with baby and snotty-nosed infant. Her shopping swings in a net bag, and three more youngsters, puffy-skinned and snotty, cling to her skirts. Too many children.

Vincent pulls out his notebook and begins to draw. He imagines this woman as the centre of an enormous mural, unwanted children teeming about her, nosepickers gobbling up the world's resources. He sketches quickly, staring misty-eyed at her departing rump. Suddenly, he runs after her.

'Stop!' he cries. His fingers founder in the soft moist flesh of her arm.

She looks at him, too weary to be surprised.

'Good woman,' he says, 'I understand your plight ... Believe me, I sympathise. Take this!' He presses the remaining copy of *Green Out of Chaos* into her hand. 'The next time your husband seeks to have his way with you, tell him to read this instead.'

She fingers the gold lettering on the spine. Mutely, she slides the book in with her shopping, next to the onions.

Vincent hurries on ahead. He feels like leaping into the air, stretching his feathery arms wide, and flying like a great bird over the rooftops. Hasn't he just resolved another of life's heartaches? He plunges into Nassau Street, where he greets the bus-load of American tourists disgorging into the college with a cheery, two-fingered salute.

In the pub it's dark and cool. Henry snaps open a newspaper between them. 'I don't want to talk,' he mutters.

Naturally, Vincent's curiosity is aroused. He notes that Henry's usually fuzzy hair is drooping, and that his skin has gone spotty. 'What's up, Henry?' he insists. 'How's tricks?'

'Would you kindly piss off, Vincent.'

'Tch, tch, manners ... And you with a show that's just sold out. Such behaviour is unworthy of Dublin's hottest artistic property. The one and only, Henry Harrison. Painter of mouths extraordinaire. Big mouths, small mouths, mouths yelling and mouths in repose. And isn't the entire town queuing up for the privilege of hanging your mouths up on their walls?' Vincent wraps an avuncular arm about Henry's shoulders. 'It should strike you as obvious, my boy,' he grins, 'that I won't let up until you tell me what's wrong.'

'All right, then,' Henry sighs. 'It's Denise. She wants to get married. Now you know. So will you please get lost?'

'Married? I don't understand. You've been shacked

up with her for ten years. Why the hell would she want to get married?'

'Success.' Henry glares into his pint. 'It's the ruination of me. She says it's a question of property. What's mine is hers anyway. But Denise wants it in writing, in case I undergo a massive change in personality.'

'Hard cheese,' Vincent says. 'And I thought she was a sensible girl, although a trifle too full in the bosom for my taste.'

'For Christsake, what do her boobs have to do with you?' Henry snarls.

'It's a question of aesthetics. She looks like she might tip over. Big boobs are a sign of instability in a woman.'

'You're an exceedingly irritating man, Vincent. If you weren't so big, I'd thump you. If I'd known you were coming here, I'd have gone some place else.'

Vincent grins. 'Come on, oul' flower. I'll buy you a jar, and we'll drink to the happy day. Besides, I'm sympathetic. I have woman troubles of my own.'

'I'm not surprised,' Henry snaps. 'The way you carry on with women is disgraceful. Though what they see in you in the first place is one of life's mysteries.'

'I'm lovable.'

'You are in my eye. You stink, Vincent. You don't wash. When you sat down beside me, I knew who it was without looking.'

'Rainwater. I wash in rainwater. Nothing's purer.'

'For Christsake, have you never heard of total immersion? I don't understand you. You've plenty of money, but you live like a tinker. You drag home rubbish off the streets ... '

'Artifacts. Grist for my mill.'

'Rubbish,' Henry insists. 'Why any woman would set

foot in your place, I don't know.'

'I look after a woman,' Vincent says with dignity. 'I make her immortal through my art.'

'Yeah. Then you kiss her goodbye. You're a hypocrite.'

'Hypocrite?' protests Vincent. 'That's hard. I'm an artist.'

Henry sneers. 'Self-deception, Vincent. You stack up women, just like you do rubbish, higher and higher, just so you can scramble on top. You're a megalomaniac, my friend, and some day some developer's going to flatten that warehouse of yours and everything that's in it. I only hope I'll be there to watch.'

'Very droll, Henry. You've a gift with words, oul' flower.' But Vincent is disconcerted. He sees Calley again, Calley on a mountain of tyres and tubing. Calley, haloed in wire and spark plugs. But he'd rather not think about her at all.

It is mid-afternoon, and Vincent is not feeling his usual happy self. He peers into the window of a fishmonger's, and sees a scene of carnage on crushed ice. Chopped and chunked, lumps of monkfish moulder next to cod and clammy haddock. The jaws of a sea trout gape at dead fans of ray. The silver-bellied mackerel tarnish before Vincent's eyes. Death everywhere. Furiously, he begins to sketch. A net full of people take shape under his pencil, people being speared on the sharp proboscis of a swordfish, dead bits everywhere. Why not glue fish scales to his work Vincent thinks, and smear it all in fish blood?

The fishmonger, rightly concerned for his custom,

materialises at Vincent's shoulder. 'Can I help you, sir?' he enquires with caution.

'You can,' Vincent grunts, without looking up. 'I'll have one of each.'

'One of each what, sir?'

'What's the matter with you?' Vincent snarls. 'Are you deaf? I want one of everything you have.'

'Will I include the crustaceans and molluscs, sir, that is one shrimp, one scallop, one mussel, one ... '

'I said everything, didn't I?' Irritably, Vincent pulls a fistful of notes out of his pocket, and waves them under the fishmonger's nose.

Weighted down with oozing, their white plastic knotted about his fingers, Vincent strides homewards, leaving a miasma of fish smell behind him. He is angry now, with so much of his day routed, and nothing accomplished. It is all Calley's fault. Calley and her progenitive nonsense. She had lain in wait for him outside a pub. Then she'd tracked him home to ravish him. The hell with her, he thinks.

Vincent stares into the canal, where the water that shimmered in the morning, now broods murkily. A metallic rod juts out from the swirling waters. Curiosity gets the better of him. Flinging his fishy bags aside, he slides down the bank, wading out into the quagmire, mud stirring beneath his toes. The treasure shudders beneath his mighty heavings. Systematically, he works it loose, until tattered leatherette, smeared in slime and brown weeds, breaks through in a maelstrom of browny-yellow water.

'A pram!' he cries. His dripping discovery totters seedily, its hood gone, a wheel missing, and its box-like body that of a coffin. On the verge, he strips the water and muck away with his bare hands. Fate, he realises, has sent him this pram for his Malthusian mural of unwanted children. He can picture his behemoth-woman shambling behind it, with its stink of rotten leaves and dead dogs.

As he works, he hears a pathetic mewing. A scabby kitten quivers on top of his bags of fish. She claws frantically at the plastic film, an insurmountable barrier to her cat-heart's desire. He can help her, Vincent O'Toole, Saviour and Superman. He tears a bag open with his teeth, spilling out the meaty flesh of a salmon. 'Good pussy,' he says, as she gorges. His heart fills with affection for the tiny creature.

He loads the remaining bags into the ramshackle pram. Hoisting kitten in his great paw of a hand, Vincent arranges her, tenderly, on a bed of plastic and fish, where she whines in ecstasy. Then, dragging the three-wheeled pram after him, Vincent shuffles homeward, the words of his favourite song drifting away into the fading light.

As we live a life of ease,
Everyone of us has all he needs:
Sky of blue and sea of green,
In our yellow submarine ...

Behind him, he leaves a trail of sludge and water like a monster snail.

Vincent stands beneath his crumbling roof, the roof through which you can see the stars. Calley is still there, but there is no longer reason to fear her. She has laid herself out upon the trestle table. She has draped herself in a sheet. Juliet on a tombstone. Her head reposes upon the pink brick. He imagines the dagger in her heart, its hilt spangled with gemstones. Dead by her own hand, Ophelia, strewn with pansies and rosemary, her curly hair cascading over the brick.

His eyes fill with tears, but he takes his sketch-book and begins to draw. It is the least he can do. Poor mad thing. He hunches his shoulders and hums. His toes jig. He puts everything he's got into the drawing. With a vibrant pencil, he catches cheekbone and marble eyelids, the undulating lines of breast, abdomen, pelvis and thigh. Tenderly, he draws her dainty feet, each milky toe opalescent in the candle light.

And as he draws, line by line, bit by bit, he comes to believe in his daughter, who will never be. He finishes the drawing and admires it. If only, he thinks ... then stops. There are straws that can only be seized once.

Once again, Vincent is hungry. He slips out to his larder, but finds no consolation there. She has vandalised his storehouse. The blank shelves mock him, stripped, their naked wood marked with hollow rings. His soldiers routed, his buttress against tomorrow smashed. Vincent's breath explodes in short, hard pants, which echo off the empty shelves.

The nearly empty shelves. Disorientated, perhaps hallucinating, Vincent sees a jar of lentils and a carton of carrot juice. He throws back his head, and roars, shaking his fist and addressing his maker. 'Why have You done this to me, God? I've always served You in my own way. Are You laughing at me?' Vincent trembles. He hears a rattling sound, and sees the empty shelves dancing before him like bones. He realises that even he will not live forever, and that when he is gone, he will leave nothing behind him.

'Would You like a glass of carrot juice, God?' he says out loud.

Laughing sardonically, he returns to Calley. His Madonna entombed. Through death she has scratched her mark upon him. She, who had mounted him like a butterfly, was strong in ways of which he'd never dreamed.

In the coffin-shaped pram, the kitten is stirring. Soon, she leaps out, cocky now with her bellyful of fish. She pads across the warehouse floor to curve up on to Calley's breast, where she coils, purring like a full-fed lioness.

Vincent considers the kitten with melancholy eyes. It seems indecent, this intimacy between life and death. Gently, he lays his hand upon her warm, furry body. Calley's eyes flutter open. 'You've brought me a kitten,' she says. 'Why, that's lovely, Vincent.' She sits up, stretches, then cuddles the kitten in her lap. 'I like the pram,' she says.

Startled, Vincent draws back. Is she real, or is he dreaming? His hand stretches out and brushes against her throat.

'I love you, Vincent,' she says. 'I love so much.' Thoughtfully he squeezes her dark curls between his fingers. This time, he believes her. Her breath is warm against his cheek.

Her wiry arm emerges from the sheet that covers her. 'Aren't these what you wanted?'

He accepts the orange socks from her hand, then sits companionably beside her on the table. Kicking off his ruined sandals, he pulls the socks she's knitted for him onto his over-sized feet.

Biddy's Research

by Moya Roddy

Biddy never took any chances. She knew there was a world-wide conspiracy. Oh sometimes men got it too but that was accidental. When this happened it was usually referred to as happening to 'people'. Biddy resented this: it made it seem as if things were evenly divided but this was not the case. Not by a long shot. She didn't have the statistics – who believed statistics anyway? Women were being killed, murdered, exterminated, call it what you will, the result was the same. So Biddy took precautions.

She never crossed a road, even at a pedestrian crossing if there was a Securicor van in the vicinity or what looked like a get-away car outside a bank. That was courting disaster. My God, she'd never realised how many banks there were in Dublin. Banks themselves were no-go areas. She corresponded with one but that was as far as it went. She refused to have gas in her home – five explosions in eight months this year alone. Electricity was so much cleaner even if it was more expensive. It's an ill-wind, she thought each time electricity prices shot up.

Cycling, swimming and jogging were all out but Biddy kept as fit as anybody running on the spot in the comfort of her own home. It also gave her more time to concentrate on her Research. She was at the stage of differentiating between the 'accidental', those that happened to people and the 'planned', those that happened to women.

Biddy sat back from her columns and chewed a

pencil. It was films that first opened her eyes. Now, Biddy loved the cinema. She loved to sit in the darkness munching popcorn, following the progress of this or that heroine, lost to the world. Little by little it dawned on her that whenever women had more than a bit part they had to die or get bumped off, even if they were the heroine. In fact, especially if they were the heroine. Psycho clinched it for her. To be completely fair (and Biddy felt this was essential to her work) the odd one survived if death by boredom didn't count. Having never been troubled by the question whether Art mirrored Life or Life Art (or indeed if Cinema was Art) Biddy allowed these little facts to hover round her subconscious until one day sitting in her comfy chair Biddy realised it wasn't only in films women were being bumped off. It was happening in real life and to the bit parts as well as the heroines!

Biddy tried her discovery out on a friend.

'I think,' she began (she was not the sort of person to force her opinions on others) 'I think women are being bumped off ... ?' Her friend looked at her a moment, agreed with her profusely, only to drag the dreaded word 'people' into the conversation within minutes.

Biddy sighed, did nobody know or care? Going back to her work she picked up the last page and read it through, shaking her head. Surely if it was a fact of life her mother would have warned her. Unless she thought Biddy might worry herself to death. She smiled. It was true she was the worrying kind and so was her mother. Now she understood why, she wished she'd been more patient with her. But at the time she had simply gone along with her father when he said, 'If your mother didn't have something to worry about, she'd make something up.' It was easy for him to talk, he wasn't an endangered species.

No sooner had Biddy inserted another piece of paper into her typewriter than she was on her feet. She felt restless. Up and down the room she paced, weaving her way in and around the endless piles of newspapers she'd accumulated. A headline caught her eye. '*Murdered After Smiling In Pub*'. She stopped pacing. It was true those responsible were not entirely heartless. If you read the papers properly and paid attention to the radio and television plenty of clues were given about what to avoid and how to make the most of your chances. Glancing at her watch she saw it was time for the news. The announcer's soothing voice lulled her as she listened absently to more news about the Middle East; further recession in America.

Then Biddy's practised ear discerned a slight change in the broadcaster's tone. Her heart quickened. Earlier this morning, he read, a woman was accidentally killed while sitting on park railings which were somehow connected to a mains supply of electricity. Biddy snorted at the word 'accidental'. Where would it all end? What would happen as she got older and her memory worsened? Would she remember all the danger areas? Would she end up trapped in her own home for fear of making a mistake? Mulling her thoughts over, Biddy went into her kitchen to make lunch. She tried not to have second thoughts about her electric cooker.

On her way to a newspaper library that afternoon Biddy ploughed through the Dublin traffic wondering again if she should move 'car accidents' to the 'planned' category. Driving a car meant she never had to walk anywhere late at night, never had to take a taxi and never never had to hitch a lift – all potentially fatal situations. It also meant she could wear what she liked, so a blouse or a skirt or the cut of her jeans could not be the cause of ending what she loved so dearly. There was another reason for driving a car which Biddy didn't like admitting. Her Research showed she had a physical defect which if not exactly lethal certainly stacked the dice against her. Her right eye had a slight nervous tick which if you didn't know could be construed as a wink. Since discovering this Biddy wore dark glasses and preferred to drive everywhere. She wasn't one to take chances especially now the Research was going so well. Biddy smiled into the rear mirror. 'I'm going to expose this conspiracy if it's the last thing I do,' she vowed.

After a hard afternoon's work Biddy left the library and returned to where she'd parked her car earlier. An empty space greeted her. Taking her glasses off she looked frantically round. The car was nowhere to be seen. Quickly she put her glasses back on realising her eye was going a mile a minute. It must have been stolen. Biddy headed for the nearest police station, thanking her lucky stars it was summer and still bright at six o'clock.

During the weeks that followed Biddy made all her appointments in the daytime and wore a boilersuit and glasses wherever she went. Despite this, her work was being held up. At Trinity (where else?) she'd uncovered the whereabouts of a woman who'd written or attempted to write a thesis on the same subject. She was now living in a Therapeutic Community and for some reason would only see women at night. A kindred spirit! Biddy needed to talk to her. But could she risk doing something she hadn't done for eight years: go on public transport alone at night?

Just this once, she argued with herself, donning a strong pair of boots and tucking her hair under a beret. Perhaps if she looked more like a person she'd be safe.

After a long discussion with Gráinne (that was the woman's name) Biddy discovered they'd both come to the same conclusion though from different directions: there were no such beings as persons or people; there were only men and women. When Biddy confided that this was the point she was stuck at, Gráinne admitted the same.

'It's probably staring us in the face,' she said and Biddy agreed. 'Sometimes', she went on, 'something is so obvious you miss it.'

Sadly they said goodbye, promising to contact one another if either felt they'd cracked it.

Walking down a dark road to the nearest bus-stop Biddy almost forgot her danger so sure was she that the solution was on the tip of her tongue. Then remembering that walking slowly could be misinterpreted, a court case had established that, she hurried along looking neither right nor left but at the same time being aware of every leaf on every tree and the slightest movement of a toffee-paper on the pavement. A woman tottering by on very high-heels gave Biddy a grateful look. Oh my God, thought Biddy, has nobody told her about footwear. She sighed. The sooner her Research was published the better.

When she reached the stop she noticed a person was already waiting there. A man, she corrected herself. She wasn't sure why but almost immediately her eye began to twitch. Thank God for her glasses. Then she admitted to herself she was afraid. The man was watching her. In fact she was sure he had moved ever so slightly in her direction. Her mouth dried. Was this it? Was this one of the exterminators? What should she do? For a moment her mind went blank, then the words of an old song her mother used to sing popped into her head ...

Whenever I feel afraid I hold myself erect
And whistle a happy tune so no one will
suspect I'm afraid.

Holding her head as erect as possible Biddy whistled. A weird sound emanated from her lips. It made her laugh loudly it was so weird. She saw the man look at her then move away. She whistled again and laughed again, then – to keep in tune – she banged on some railings, quite forgetting the lunchtime news. He probably thinks I'm mad, she thought. Maybe they're afraid of mad people, I mean women. She laughed again as the bus came.

Biddy stared from the lighted bus. I've survived, she said to herself, then her heart somersaulted. The answer she was looking for was as plain as the darkness outside. For a moment she couldn't believe it. It was too obvious for words. But after a moment she had to accept it was the only possible explanation. Her Research was over. She sat for a moment relishing her discovery. Then for the first time in eight years Biddy smiled openly in a public place at night.

Just wait 'till I phone Gráinne, she thought.

The Garden of Eden

by Éilís Ní Dhuibhne

In the end, David simply said, 'I am going.' And Carmelita knew what he meant.

'All right,' she replied. She had been waiting for this announcement for twelve years. She had feared it, postponed it, protested against it, and also – at other times, of course – wanted it, craved it, paved the way for it. Now – this now, this minute, sitting, appropriately, at the kitchen table (ad mensa. What's the Latin for 'at'? She wondered idly) – it was nothing but a bald fact, like the sun that shone on the lawn outside, like the marigold in the window-box, like the wine-glass of water on the blue checked cloth.

David stood up, leaving a little food on his plate, and went upstairs. Carmelita sat, gazing absently out the window. The laburnum was dropping black pods on the yard. The lobelia had withered. A few montbretiae bloomed with their characteristic brilliance in the euphemistically-named rockery but mostly the garden was on the wane. Middle August, and hardly a thing left in it. After nine years in the house. And garden. David usually took care of the garden. The split would be mainly *ad hortis*, actually, she thought calmly, pleased to remember this word, if not its cases. He'd never done anything much at the table except eat the food she'd cooked.

Carmelita considered the garden next door as she often did. It was the horticultural *tour de force* of the neighbourhood: tender velvet lawn, bright but not gaudy borders, shrubs in all the right corners, flowering or leafing in a happy sequence of colours, scents and textures. Patio, arbour, roses clambering over trellis, geraniums in great carved terracotta pots. An ornate Victorian conservatory.

Carmelita envied them, those next door. She coveted that garden. She craved it passionately.

David popped his head in and said: 'I'm off now. Goodbye!' His heavy step sounded on the hall floor. The door opened and then shut slowly and sadly, but firmly.

Carmelita stopped thinking about the garden next door. She got up and plugged in the kettle and made a cup of tea. When it was ready, she carried it out to the garden, her own garden, and sat down at the table there. A white plastic table with a green sun umbrella, and a few odd, mismatched lawnchairs surrounding it. She sat and looked at her shrubs, her flowers, her trees, and the sky. The evening sky in early autumn, the middle ages of the year. The little bit she could see in the gap between the sycamores was a pale wishy-washy pink. The sun had already disappeared behind the roofs of the houses on the next road. The summer is over, well and truly over, she thought and a dreadful last-rose-of-summer sentiment of loss and bereavement overwhelmed her for a few minutes. But she did not wallow in it; she waited for it to pass, because she was so accustomed to this sensation.

Periodically, every year from about the tenth of August to the beginning of September it struck. Her last-rose-of-summer depression – she was very sensitive to seasonal cycles, like a lot of women who live in suburbs. The beginning of nice ones, like spring or summer, brought jubilance. The end of nice ones – and there is only one season that really ends – was like a great tragedy which experience seemed to exaggerate rather than assuage. And August seemed much more of an ending, so much gloomier, than September, which had its own character and self-confidence and was the beginning of something again, even if it was something not very good. School. Frost. Long dark nights.

Carmelita and David had been married for twelve years. Oh yes! How time flew. It seemed no length at all since their wedding. Since that time of being in love with David. Perhaps time does not exist where the emotions are concerned. On the other hand it was aeons ago; its trappings belonged to history. That ceremony in the registry office in Kildare Street. The drinks afterwards in the Shelbourne, with everyone dressed up. Somehow the bridesmaid in white pants and a navy striped tee-shirt had looked odd, certainly. Carmelita could have killed her. But most of them had made a respectable effort with flowery dresses and hats. Outmoded. Dated. Ancient.

David had been as always: smiling broadly, jocular and in full control. He was smart and quick-witted, David. She had basked in that, in his protection. He was never at a loss. His decisions were, almost invariably, the correct ones. And he never regretted them, as a matter of principle.

The decision to get married had not been his, of course, but hers. And her decisions were frequently wrong, she had found out as her life progressed. Usually they were irrational, whereas David's would as a rule be the opposite. It had seemed terribly necessary to marry him at that time twelve years ago, though. She had been pregnant, but that was not why. It had seemed necessary before the pregnancy, which was an effect, not a cause, of the need. Marriage to David had seemed to be her only salvation, the only course open to her in life. Life without him, she thought, was unthinkable. She would die without him. She would wither up and cease to exist.

And indeed her expectations had been fulfilled. Marriage had brought happiness and activity. Life had been full as a tick. It ticked, ticked all day, all night. There was never a moment's idleness. She had been so busy, so very busy, for several years. So busy that she had not had time to consider whether she was happy or not.

Only in retrospect did she realise how happy she had been during that hectic time. Not having time to think of it, that had been her happiness, it seemed. Not having time to bless herself.

She was not busy anymore.

The garden was empty before her eyes. Friday evening. She had the weekend free, three nights, two whole days, all for herself.

She walked over to the fence dividing her garden from the garden of Eden. She did this every night, because the neighbours were away on their fortnight's holiday in Greece. There was a broken place on the fence – God knows how they had let it remain broken – over which she could peer and get a perfect view.

The first sight of it broke upon her like a peaceful oriental vision: there was a quietness in this garden, partly because it *was* quiet since there was nobody in it, but more because of its perfection. The greenest grass. The fluid forms of the bushes. The pale pinks, yellows, lilacs of the flowers. It was in no way a busy garden, although it required much business to achieve the effect it created. Like a beautiful, rich room, upon which endless attention and expense has been lavished, it looked natural and spontaneous.

David had driven off in the car. She had heard him starting it, she remembered, just after the door shut. He was possibly far away by now. The thought that there was no longer a car crossed her mind, like a slight shadow, and disappeared. Who needs a car?

She began to climb the fence. A thin wooden fence. It was not difficult, because it had wires attached to it, bits of broken chicken wire up which she had once tried to grow woodbine but without success.

She swung herself over the narrow top and jumped onto the pale red pavingstones of the patio next door. At first she stood and looked around at everything she had seen so often from the other side of the fence. The palm and elephant grass just where the patio met the lawn. The green hose lying on the slabs. The pots of deeply pink geraniums all around. And, placed at interesting vantage points further down the garden, beds of lupins, hollyhocks, columbines and Canterbury bells, their colours deep and velvet, their heads bowing, one to the other, like coquettish ladies at some brilliantly flirtatious court. She breathed deeply, and perfume from mignonette, honeysuckle and escallonia filled her lungs, along with a headier, more intoxicating air: something like incense.

She walked slowly along the lawn. The greenness of it soaked into her skin; she could feel her body absorbing it. It was like swimming softly, breast-stroking through a long aquamarine pool. Or through a cloud. Although naturally she had never swum in a cloud.

She sat on the grass for a minute. It was dampish. She could feel the wet seeping into her skirt. A ladybird came and crawled along her leg, one of the more unusual yellow ladybirds which, in their gay spotted shells, reminded Carmelita of fashionably rigged-out toddlers. It was a great year for these insects. All the gardens were infested with them. They were tolerated even by the best gardeners on account of their appetite for greenflies. All years were great years for greenfly.

Carmelita stayed on the grass for a long time. Then she got up and left using the same route and technique she'd employed in entry. Before she left she cut three slips from the geraniums, whose pink blossoms rested like hot fluttering butterflies on their turgid foliage. And when she got to her own side of the fence, she potted the slips in terracotta plastic pots, in peat moss, and put them on the window-sill to root. She had heard from a woman she'd met once on a plane to London that stolen slips did best.

She went to bed.

The house creaked a lot. Some doors banged because a window was open. She thought about burglars. She believed in burglars, but her image of them, like her childhood images of God and the Devil, was vague. They were male, they would break glass, they would burst into her bedroom and ...

Lulled by such creaks and bangs and ideas, she fell asleep.

The next day would have been long and empty, had she not decided in the morning that she really must go shopping. So she took the bus into the city centre and spent the whole day walking around the shops, trying on clothes, examining furniture and rugs. Time passes very quickly in town, and she remembered the Saturdays of her youth, her later youth that is, when she had lived with her mother and had her job, the job she still had. Shop after shop, garment after garment. Bought, worn a few times, discarded.

She bought a white linen suit. And a bag of peaches. And a packet of incense sticks.

And several small terracotta pots.

That evening, she watched television and cut three slips of escallonia in the garden next door.

She burned the incense, thinking how David hated incense or anything that seemed cheap and eastern, like curried eggs and the novels of Hesse and Indian rugs. She drank some red wine but it was sour as it usually is if you buy a cheap bottle in a supermarket and she could not take more than one glass.

Her thoughts were less of burglars as she lay in bed, and more of the past. Not the past with David, which hardly seemed like past. But of her childhood, of her teenage years which seemed, in retrospect, serene and carefree. She also thought about her slips and planned the future of her garden. Every mickle makes a muckle, she thought, and eventually it will look like theirs next door. Patience is a virtue.

Carmelita was not an especially patient woman, and on Sunday she went to a garden centre and bought a palm tree and a blue hydrangea (she'd never fancied the pink) and came home and planted them on the back lawn. And that night, after dark, she stole a large carved terracotta pot from the garden next door. But for the time being she put it in her bedroom where the next-door neighbours were not likely to see it.

That night as she lay in bed she thought of the next-door neighbours. They would not have seen the pot if she'd put it in the hall or the living-room either, she thought, because they did not visit her house. The reason was, she and David had had such fearful rows in the year or two after the accident. Carmelita had been given to screaming loudly in the middle of the night. She used to accuse David of all kinds of awful things: not being sensitive, not caring about her, not giving her the love she needed. She had ranted and raved and screamed at the top of her voice, and sometimes David had hit her. To shut her up. Battered. She had been a battered wife, according to a certain point of view. In her own estimation, in retrospect but even at the time, she could justify David's hitting her. They always say they've been provoked. But in his case it was, she suspected, true. Anyway invariably she had hit him back, and not infrequently she had hit him first. They had been like two boys scuffling in the school playground.

Except that the sound effects were higher pitched and more alarming.

They heard. She knew they must have heard. It was so embarrassing. She hadn't wanted to speak to them. She didn't speak to them, or have cups of tea with them, or invite them in for a drink on Christmas Eve.

It had all stopped long ago. There was no noise, no

screaming. No fighting at all. But the pattern was set. No neighbourliness. No visits.

Lulled by these thoughts she fell asleep.

The next morning was Monday and Carmelita was supposed to get up and go to work. She worked in a bank. She was a cashier. It was not as boring to her now as it had been when she'd started it: she enjoyed saying hello to the customers, she liked to be nice and friendly and make them feel at ease, which is not how most people feel in a bank. And also, over the years, she had grown fond of her colleagues and of her salary.

But this morning she did not go to work. She got up at the usual time of eight o'clock and went down and had her coffee. But when the time for leaving the house came, she did not go. Instead she went into the garden. She examined the slips: none of them had withered so far, which she took to be a good sign. Now she had fuchsia, escallonia, and geraniums on the go. She climbed over the fence and looked around. The garden next door looked even more wonderful than usual in the early morning light. The fresh clean sunshine, the unsullied air of start of day, suited its own spic-and-span, cared-for, character. It was in its element.

Carmelita walked all around it, simply admiring. She no longer felt any envy or covetousness, she realised, and supposed it must be because she knew that soon – or at least eventually – she was going to have her own beautiful garden. As beautiful as this. Or more beautiful? No. Just the same.

What would she take? She remembered that they were due home the day after tomorrow, so her time in the garden was limited, and she would have to choose exactly what she wanted now. She looked at dahlias, and lupins, and tea roses. Broom and rose of sharon and a shrub she did not know the name of, which had greenish reddish leaves and huge fluffy red balls. She looked at elephant grass and marram grass and coeur de lion.

In the end, she cried 'Ah!' Because she saw it. Just exactly what she had wanted all the time. How odd that she had not seen it before; how very odd. In the corner of the patio, propped up against the wall, a small tricycle belonging to the youngest child next door. There were three children, two girls and a boy. The boy was the youngest. He was four, and this was his bicycle.

She grabbed it and let it down over the fence as gently as she could. Then she herself climbed over, and carried the tricycle up to her bedroom, where she put it on the floor just beside the bed.

After the accident, all Raymond's things had been given away. Absolutely everything: David had thought it was better that way. It was all as bad as it could be. They didn't need reminders, he had said, packing the toys and the clothes and things, Raymond's things, into boxes for the travellers who called to the door every Saturday, regular as clockwork.

There were the photographs, of course, but only in albums. None out on the sideboard, none displayed with the other photographs on the mantelpiece. They had to get over it. They had to forget.

She lay in bed for a while, thinking about her slips and glancing at the tricycle from time to time. Then she searched in the drawers of David's desk for the albums. She selected three of the nicest pictures, showing Raymond at one, three and seven-and-a-half, just after he'd made his First Communion and just before he'd died. She propped them up on her dressing table where she could see them at night before going to sleep and in the morning as soon as she awoke. She'd get some frames for them later. Later today, or maybe tomorrow, or maybe she'd ask David to get them.

Because of course he was going to come back. And David came back that very night, because he'd rung the office and she hadn't been there, and because he couldn't cook, and for various other reasons. His decisions were usually rational, David's, and usually correct. And he never regretted them. On principle.

About the Authors

Maeve Binchy was born in 1940 and grew up in Dalkey near Dublin where she has her home today. A columnist with the *Irish Times* for many years, she is an international bestselling author. Her short story collections include *London Transport, The Lilac Bus, Dublin 4,* and *Silver Wedding.* Her novels include *Light a Penny Candle, Echoes, Firefly Summer, Circle of Friends* and *The Copper Beech.* Her stage plays include *End of Term* and *Half Promised Land.* Her television play *Deeply Regretted By* won two Jacobs Awards and the best script award at the Prague Film Festival. Much of her work has also been made into highly successful films.

Máiríde Woods was born in Dublin in 1948. Brought up in the Glens of Antrim, she has lived mainly in Dublin since she was sixteen. She has won two Hennessy Literary Awards and the Francis McManus Short Story Competition. A number of her plays have been performed on radio and she won the Wexford Women's Poetry Competition. Currently doing a masters degree in Equality Studies at University College Dublin, she teaches creative writing and is currently working on new short stories.

Moy McCrory was born in Liverpool in 1953 and grew up in the Irish community there. She was educated there and in Belfast and now lives in Salisbury. She has published *The Waters Edge,* followed by *Bleeding Sinners,* and *Those Sailing Ships of his Boyhood Dreams* (all short stories). She has also published a novel *The Fading Shrine* and has just finished a play for the Breakout company which will be performed in schools. Currently working on a new novel, she also teaches creative writing in the UK and Germany.

Angela Bourke was born in Dublin in 1952. The director of the M Phil programme in Irish Studies at University College Dublin, she is currently visiting professor of Celtic languages and literatures at Harvard University. The author of *Caoineadh na dTrí Muire*, a book about women's religious oral poetry in Irish, she is currently working on a collection of short stories. Angela is one of the eight panel editors for the fourth volume of the Field Day Anthology of Irish Writing.

Anne Enright was born in Dublin in 1962. She was educated there and in Canada and now lives in Dublin. She has worked in fringe theatre as an actress and writer and is now a producer/director in RTE. Her short story collection *The Portable Virgin* was published in 1991, the year in which she was awarded The Rooney Prize for Irish Literature. She was also shortlisted along with two other writers for the *Irish Times*/Aer Lingus Irish Literature Prize in fiction in 1992.

Liz McManus was born in Canada in 1947. She grew up in Ireland and having qualified as an architect worked in various parts of the country. She is now a member of the Irish Parliament (Dáil) for the Democratic Left party. Her first novel *Acts of Submission* was published in 1991. She has received a Hennessy Literary Award, an Irish Pen Short Story Award and a Listowel Short Story Prize.

Mary Dorcey was born and brought up in Dublin. She has lived in various parts of Ireland and has travelled extensively including France, England, America and Japan. Her first collection of poems *Kindling* was published in 1982 and was followed by another volume called *Not Everyone Sees This Night*. She was awarded a Rooney Prize for Irish Literature in 1990. Her first collection of stories *A Noise from the Woodshed* was published in 1989 followed in 1992 by a collection of poetry called *Moving into the Space Cleared by Our Mothers*.

Clairr O'Connor was born in Limerick in 1951 and now lives in Maynooth, Co. Kildare. A secondary school teacher, her novel *Belonging* was published in 1991. She also published a book of poetry called *When You Need Them*. Both her plays *Bodies* and *The Annulment* were performed at the Cork Arts Theatre and she has written a number of radio plays. She is currently working on a second novel.

Trudy Hayes was born in Nigeria of Irish parents in 1962 but has lived in Dublin since she was two. She is the author of a pamphlet in the Attic Press LIP series called *The Politics of Seduction*, in which she explores the area of sexual politics. She writes short stories and drama and her play *Out of My Head* was performed in Dublin in 1992. Currently working as writer-in-residence with a company called the Down to Earth Theatre Company for Children, she has just finished a collection of stories and a play called *The No Praise Man.*

Mary Morrissy was born in Dublin in 1957, where she still lives. A staff journalist — and regular book reviewer — with *The Irish Times*, her first collection of short stories *A Lazy Eye* has just been published. Winner of a Hennessy Literary Award, she used an Arts Council bursary which she received in 1992 to spend some time in Italy writing.

Ivy Bannister was born in New York in 1951 and has lived in Ireland for over twenty years. She has twice won the Francis McManus Competition and a Hennessy Literary Award for short stories. Her plays have been performed on radio and read in various theatres around Ireland. Her play the *Wild Circus Show* won an O. Z. Whitehead Award; she has also won a Listowel Writers Week Award and a P. J. O'Connor Radio Play Award. She lectures part-time on drama and literature.

Moya Roddy was born in Dublin. Having lived for much of her adult life in England she has now settled in Co. Galway. Her novel *The Long Way Home* was published in 1992. A screenwriter, her major work to date was a four part series for Channel 4 on family photography, but most of her work in this area has been on the fictional front and she has sold options on a number of screenplays to Hollywood. She is now working on a new novel and a screenplay.

Éilís Ní Dhuibhne was born in Dublin in 1954 and has lived there most of her life, interspersed with short spells living in Scandinavia. She works as an assistant keeper in the National Library of Ireland. Her first collection of short stories *Blood and Water* in 1989 was followed by a novel *The Bray House* in 1990 and a further collection of short stories called *Eating Women is not Recommended* was published in 1991. She writes poetry and is a published author of children's books. Éilís gives creative writing workshops, is a committee member of the Irish Writers Union and apart from working on a new novel, is also currently selecting material for the folklore section of the forthcoming additional volume to the *Field Day Anthology of Irish Writing*.